WITCH'S REVENGE

Steve stood up and moved over to the window and stared at the sky. It wasn't clear blue anymore and a small gathering of dark clouds had appeared. He examined them as he said, "But who is the Virgin Child? Did he tell you that?"

The cloud formation was definitely odd. It was moving before his eyes.

"No," Anna said. "I don't think Lady Eva shared that with him."

"Come look at these clouds, Anna," Steve said. "They're forming a symbol."

Anna wheeled herself over and looked out. She screamed and started wheeling back quickly.

Steve looked at her and then back at the pentagram drawn in the tight, ugly black clouds.

Suddenly, lightning flashed, crashed through the window and hit Anna. The bolt hit her in the stomach and ripped up her middle in a smoking blue light. The sickening smell of electrically charged flesh cloyed the room.

Then another lightning bolt struck and fried Anna's head.

HORROR FROM HAUTALA

WITCHCRAFT

Bill Michaels

Zebra Books
Kensington Publishing Corp.
http://www.zebrabooks.com

ZEBRA BOOKS are published by

Kensington Publishing Corp.
850 Third Avenue
New York, NY 10022

First Printing: March, 1997
10 9 8 7 6 5 4 3 2 1

Printed in the United States of America

For
Sharon Jarvis

ACKNOWLEDGMENTS

Special thanks to: Kevin Carney who did the first read on this book; John Scognamiglio, who is my editor, a man who truly has the patience of a saint; and Sharon Jarvis, my agent, who does what good agents do.

One

STEVE BROGAN

The distant sound of the helicopter rotors broke the morning quiet of the mountain lake just as Steve Brogan cast his line out into the water. He glanced quickly at the approaching black dot in the sky. It disappeared behind the surrounding granite peaks for a moment, then flew into sight through a gap in the jagged mountain range, and kept coming towards the lake, skimming just above the tops of the tall pine trees.

Steve looked back out at the water and let his line sink deeper, hoping his premonition was wrong. After all, what could be so important that they would send a chopper for him?

He reeled in the slack and propped the pole against a rock, then poured himself a fresh cup of coffee from his thermos. It can't be for me, he thought, and took a sip. He let the coffee warm him as he watched the black dot become a form—a black Bell Ranger with two orange stripes across the aft of the body. A private ship.

The chopper banked to the left, and for a moment Steve's hopes for solitude were raised. Then the noisy thing came around, bearing down on the private lake. In minutes it was skimming the periphery of the near-deserted lakeshore, searching, pressing the crisp morning air down, flattening the water.

"You're scaring all the fish!" Steve shouted futilely, then sat down on a rock and waited. Soon they spotted him; the helicopter suddenly made a beeline across the lake towards Steve and stopped in front of him, hanging up there like some giant wasp, one hundred feet offshore.

The rotorwash blew against his body, pushing back his auburn hair. The noise of the aircraft assaulted his ears, yet he treated it as if it were a minor distraction, took another sip of coffee, and tried to make out faces. He could see two figures with headsets, and that was it.

"Steve, is that you?" blared a woman's voice over the chopper's bullhorn.

Her voice sounded familiar, but he couldn't quite place it. And he thought he understood why she couldn't be sure of his identity. He was sitting down and had aviator sunglasses on. If he stood up, she'd recognize him for sure, even with the tan fishing vest over the red plaid Pendleton, and him wearing his blue jeans, and leather work boots. It was his size. At six-four, two hundred and ten pounds, he stood out in crowds, and most assuredly alone in a green forest. He tested his theory, and stood up.

"Oh, Steve, it *is* you! It's Veronica Dest!"

Senator Veronica Dest? What in the hell was she doing here?

"We'll park this thing somewhere, and I'll be right down. Save some fish for me. I *love* to fish."

The chopper powered up, banking right and inland, then disappeared over tall pine trees.

Ten minutes later Steve watched the senator pick her way through dense undergrowth and emerge onto a well-worn deer path that led down to the lake.

"You took the hard way," said Steve. "And you're a little overdressed for the forest, wouldn't you say?"

She stopped and looked down at her charcoal grey suit skirt and jacket. Her brown hair was cut short and done up beautifully, complementing the perfect oval of her face, and her rich brown eyes. Her white blouse had ruffles up the front, which was closed at the neck by a large obsidian oval pin. She braced herself against a pine with one hand, brought one foot up at a time and brushed the trail dust off her grey patent-leather high heels. "Thank you," she said "I have to be at a fund-raiser in Los Angeles this afternoon. Otherwise, I'd be dressed like a lumberjack like you."

Steve took the windbreaker he'd been wearing

earlier and spread it over a small boulder. "You can sit there," he said.

She offered her hand first. He shook it briefly, knowing that all the friendly talk up to now was to warm him up. Although Veronica's tone of voice was that of a personal friend, Steve knew her only as a matter of business. He wasn't quite sure if he liked her or not, either. He thought her as honest as any politician could be, and still stay in office, but he had always had an uneasy feeling around people who depended on equivocation of point of view to keep their jobs. And Steve had seen Veronica campaign: rhetoric was her long suit; her negotiating skills her trump card. And what the hell was she doing up here ruining his vacation in the first place?

"So, why are you here?" he asked bluntly.

The senator sat on the rock and stared out at the placid lake. "I need to call in a favor," she said.

"We're all even on favors, Senator," Steve replied.

"What about the Balatta Sting, Steve. I got Ken Anderson off on that weapons charge. Saving his license constitutes a favor, doesn't it? Hand grenades and rocket launchers, Steve, remember? Ken could have served time for that."

"The weapons were necessary. Balatta was big-time drugs, and a ruthless killer to boot." He turned his eyes from her and gazed across the lake to the tall pines and the granite mountains behind. It was to get away from people like the senator that he came up to these mountains. She was misrepresenting the facts, and she knew it— a negotiating ploy. God, how he hated this bullshit.

"Well," she prodded.

"That 'favor,' " Steve replied, "was wiped out by a little campaign 'intelligence' that put you over in the last election, Senator. You were trailing badly before that. Remember?" He mocked her in his emphasis of the last word. "So stop dancing around the campfire and get to what you want."

She sighed, and offered a tentative smile. "You can't blame me for trying, Steve." When he didn't respond, she continued. "Let's just say that someone I owe a favor to is calling it in— and it involves you. It's a simple matter really, something that could be cleaned up in a week, I imagine."

Steve shifted on the rock to face her. "I administrate now, Veronica. Ken runs the investigative end of the company for me. And when a United States senator happens by in the middle of the wilderness, the matter is never simple. If you want, I can have someone in my company take care of the matter . . ."

"No," she said, waving the idea off with one small hand. "The party in question was emphatic that you handle it personally. I told her there were better people around, but she wanted you."

11

Steve laughed at her jab at him. He got up and reeled in the line, and checked his bait.

"You're using miniature marshmallows?"

"These trout love 'em," Steve said, baiting the hook with a fresh tiny marshmallow. He started to cast.

"May I?"

Steve handed her the pole, not expecting much, but she surprised him, a perfect cast.

"So, you do fish."

She watched the line sink, then cranked the reel, taking up the slack. She sat back down, holding the pole. "Steve, does the name Carlotta Chalmers ring a bell?"

"Not at all."

"Doesn't surprise me. She's one of these very influential people that stays behind the scenes, but that makes things happen. She shuns publicity. She's helped me in the past, and I owe her . . . let me rephrase that, although I do owe her a big favor, I also *want* to help her. She has asked specifically for you, so I'm asking you to take the case."

"It's the publicity," Steve said, feeling an old irritation being rubbed raw for the umpteenth time.

"Off the Balatta Sting, is that what you're going to say? I know. You think she's just some rich bitch that wants 'the very best,' and that means whoever's best in the news. Well, that's not the case, Steve. It's not her style. But, whatever her reason, I'm asking you to take the case." She squirmed uncomfortably, as if the words that would follow would kill her: "As a favor to me, collectible in the future."

Steve searched her face. She was giving him her "I-am-being-open-and-honest" look. For whatever reason this meant a lot to her. It would have to, he figured, for her to have browbeat someone in his office to confess where he was, then to fly up and find him instead of waiting until he returned. This must be some powerful woman, this Carlotta Chalmers.

Evidently the senator had seen something she liked in his expression, because she offered a pleased smile. "You're too young for retirement, anyway," she said.

"Thirty-seven isn't young," said Steve. "And I'm not retired. I administrate."

"Hah!" she snorted. "You hide behind that 'I administrate.' " She paused for a moment, then shook her head. "I don't understand you. You build one of the top investigative companies in the country, and then you put yourself in a caretaker role.

"It's the Balatta Sting, isn't it? Well, there's still time to come out of retirement. It's been over a year since the Sting. It was a dangerous case. People die in such matters. It's too bad, but it's true."

Yeah, people die, thought Steve. Good people die: three good friends, among the many. And then of course, there was another sort of death—the divorce.

13

The electronic and print media had had a ball with it all. The case, dubbed The Balatta Sting by the press, had been sensational, involving top government officials, international rich-and-famous types, big money, and big drugs. The body count had been high, too. And after it was all over, Constance had left him, taking her children from a previous marriage with her—two boys he had grown to love after five years of marriage.

Of course, just as the media had blown the case out of proportion, they spread his divorce all over the nation too, so that he became not only a hero, but a tragic figure, as well. For a while there, he couldn't even walk around in public without getting cornered by some nosy stranger, and quizzed about his personal life.

The publicity was good for business, though. Offers for work poured into Brogan and Associates, all of them wanting *the* Steve Brogan working on the case. Steve switched himself to administration and told Ken Anderson to take over the investigative section. The tabloids, in the aftershocks of the case, sensationalized his change in roles. Steve remembered two headlines specifically: *STING'S BROGAN—THE LIVING CASUALTY,* and, *BALATTA STING'S HERO STUNG BY MATE.* Beside each of these was a thoroughly doctored picture showing Steve with an anguished expression on his face.

And yet, with all the hoopla about the case and the divorce, only he and Constance knew

the real reason for her leaving him—the betrayal
. . .

"Steve," said the senator.

"I'm sorry," he said. "What's it about? What's her problem?"

"Carlotta's sister's grave was violated. She wants to find out who did it, and have them brought to justice."

Something in the senator's twisted facial expression made Steve ask, "How violated?"

"Very," she said. Her expression soured even more, and Steve let the subject drop for the moment.

"You've got a nibble," he said pointing to the pole. The tip danced sharply.

She dipped the pole to the water, then jerked up. She'd hooked her fish. The pole bent over in a parabolic arch, so she lowered the tip and began to crank the reel.

"You'll take the case, then?" she asked.

"Why didn't she put the squeeze on the police if she's such a shaker and a mover?"

"She did. They drew a blank."

"I may draw a blank, too."

"You'll take it, then?"

"I'll talk to her."

"Great. I made an appointment for you for tomorrow afternoon at four. Will that be convenient?"

"No. But I can make it." Steve picked up the hand net. "You really know how to shoot holes in a vacation, don't you?"

"I don't even get a real vacation."

Steve stood beside her holding the net out over the water as she reeled frantically. Why was he taking this case? he wondered. Was it because in some part he thought she was right, he had been hiding?

He shook off the question, leaned closer to her, and asked for the second time that morning, "How violated?"

Caught up in reeling in her fish, her voice sounded almost light: "Well, for one thing, they ripped off her head and put it on upside down . . . and for another, they stole her hands."

Steve grimaced, then he knelt down, and netted the fish the senator had caught.

Two

MRS. CHALMERS

The mountain serenity of yesterday seemed a million years ago to Steve as he fought traffic up Topanga Canyon Boulevard, in Chatsworth, California, a suburb of Los Angeles.

He checked his watch: twenty to four. His appointment was at four o'clock. He should be right on time if he could find the place.

He picked up the Thomas Brothers map book off the car seat and tried to drive and read the turn-off on the map at the same time. There it was, Randy Canyon Road. And he was just on it. He made the turn, and kept on driving, watching the higher-priced tract homes give way to more rural ranch style homes with a few acres of land, and finally into open land. As he gazed out at the fields he thought about how varied Los Angeles County was, encompassing mountains and beach property, heavy-duty city life to nice unspoiled areas like this. But somewhere around here was the Chalmers house. The road curved and there he saw it—

Damn, how did that get out here? he wondered. Someone built it, of course, he answered himself, but it just seemed out of place out here in the middle of this undeveloped area.

And even though he hadn't reached the drive, he knew it was the Chalmers mansion. The huge old Victorian manse stood three stories high, in great repair, painted white with green trim. Ten dormer windows poked out of the front roof; the porch ran the length of the house, and was ornate with gingerbread and columns, yet appeared open and airy, and welcoming.

A fence of high brick columns supporting rows of black wrought-iron spears, surrounded the entire estate.

Bucks, Steve thought. Big bucks.

He turned into the drive and passed under a black wrought-iron arch that read CHALMERS, and through the open gate. He followed a long stretch of concrete drive that cut a swath through several acres of neatly manicured lawn and bushes up to a circle drive in front of the house.

A black stretch limousine sat unattended in front of the car barn, and parked to the side of the house was a plumber's truck.

Suddenly, a man in overalls ran out of the house and jumped in the truck and peeled out onto the drive. He was forced to slow down to pass safely by Steve's Cadillac on the drive. "Hey, buddy," he yelled at Steve, "look out the

fuckin' dogs, man! Look out the fuckin' dogs!"
and drove on past gaining speed as he approached the gate.

Steve didn't see any dogs, but as he parked
in front of the house he did spy two cute little
girls by a distant peach tree pulling Cabbage
Patch dolls around in a red wagon on the lawn.
They looked over at him and the older one
waved tentatively.

Steve raised his hand in return and mounted
the stairs to the porch. One of the two mahogany doors opened and a huge Samoan man in
his late twenties greeted him. "Mr. Brogan?
Yes?"

Steve nodded, noting the slight accent in the
man's voice.

"Ah, good. I'm Motu, Mrs. Chalmers's personal secretary." He offered his hand. Steve
shook it and was led inside into a large entryway. He craned his neck and looked up at where
the banistered stairway terminated, two more
floors above. "Hate to take a dive from up
there," he said to Motu.

Motu looked up. "I always walk close to the
wall, myself," he said with such a serious voice
that it wasn't until Steve had followed Motu into
the sitting room that he realized the big Samoan
had made a joke.

The room looked like a parlor that had been
pulled from the eighteenth century: hardwood
floors and Persian rugs, dark burnished wood
and upholstered furniture, cut crystal, and deli-

cate ceramics. Motu indicated one of two Queen Ann chairs that sat in a group with a settee and low burnished chestnut coffee table near the hearth of a large fireplace. Steve sat down.

"Mrs. Chalmers will be with you in a few minutes, Mr. Brogan. Would you like some coffee, or, tea?"

"No, thank you."

Motu offered a smile and slight bow and left.

Steve heard the little girls giggling outside, and the grandfather clock striking four Westminster Abbey chimes, and the click of dog toenails on the hardwood floor behind him. There were two sets of toenail sounds behind him that turned to thunking sounds as the feet hit the Persian rugs. Steve sat tall in his chair as two forms cruised by him one on either side.

The dogs.

Look out the fuckin' dogs! the plumber had yelled.

They were giant black and white harlequin Great Danes. They walked in unison to a point about six feet from him, then turned around and sat at attention, studying him with steady blue eyes.

There wasn't much else to do but sit still. "Hi, fellas," he finally offered, and both dogs stood up and walked to him and put their heads on his lap.

Steve smiled and cautiously put a hand on each of their big, heavy heads. "Big fellas, just like me," he said, now relaxing, enjoying the short-haired warmth under his hands. "That ol' plumber just had you guys wrong, right?"

"Wrong, Mr. Brogan."

Steve turned his head and wondered how long the woman had been standing there. He had the feeling that she had come in with the dogs. He tried to stand, but was blocked by the dogs' heads in his lap. "Back boys," he said.

"Cort, Jekk," the woman's voice cut the air with command. *"Debas-ba!"*

Steve felt the weighty heads lift, and he stood up as the dogs returned to sit at attention on the rug. "Mrs. Chalmers," he said and offered his hand. She took it, and he was struck by the warmth of the small delicate hand. She looked him straight in the eye with blue, intelligent eyes. He thought he had never seen anyone with as much personal force as this woman. Everything about her seemed to complement that impression. Her hair was fine and white and coifed around her head like a crown, her nose and features chiseled and noble. Now Steve could understand why Veronica Dest had gone to all the trouble to get this woman what she wanted. She exuded power, but without the arrogance that sometimes accompanies it.

"Please sit down," said Mrs. Chalmers.

Steve waited for the woman to be seated herself, then sat down.

She cleared her throat, then said, "Cort and Jekk," she indicated the dogs with a casual flip of her hand, "chased the plumber out. After he

21

was gone, I looked into the tool box he left behind and found two of my silver candle holders. The dears are good judges of character, Mr. Brogan. For instance, you are a private eye—" She stopped and studied him briefly. "I'm sorry. What did I say that offended you?"

She's good, thought Steve. He prided himself on being able to keep a stone face, but she'd been able to tell somehow. He couldn't deny it, she would know it was a lie.

"I'm not really offended," he said. "Just a quirk most investigators have about being called 'private eye.' We prefer 'private investigator' . . ." Steve let his voice trail off, as he drowned in his own pool of embarrassment. He never realized how petty a quirk could sound until he had to explain it to someone.

"To continue," she said, "you, as a private investigator surprise me by not carrying a gun. If you had been, Cort or Jekk would have let me know."

Trained to smell gun oil, thought Steve.

"But they are more than just security," continued Mrs. Chalmers, "they sense the inner man—their heads in your lap indicate that you are a kind man, and someone to be trusted."

"Thank you. My parents think so, anyway."

Mrs. Chalmers smiled richly, showing near-perfect teeth. "A sense of humor, too. How nice. Now, to business: I talked with Veronica, and she told me that she interrupted your vacation. That is unfortunate, and I will not forget your

22

sacrifice in helping me. I did try reaching you by normal means, but Mr. Anderson insisted that you were . . . 'out of the game' is how I believe he put it."

Steve nodded. "I'm glad to be of service. How can I help you?"

For the first time since they'd been talking Steve noticed Mrs. Chalmers become uncomfortable. She shifted almost imperceptibly in her chair and began: "Actually, two things. Unrelated. The first . . . my sister died some years ago. Three months ago, some horrible, sick people, desecrated not only her grave, but her body as well. The police have done as much as they can do, but I want those people found and punished."

"Do you remember the name of the detective on the case?"

"Yes, it was Brandeise. Timothy Brandeise."

Steve flipped a small leather notebook out of his coat pocket and pulled a pen from his shirt. He wrote down the detective's name, then kept his pen poised to make notes as he talked with her. He asked the standard questions: name of her sister? Was she married? Did Mrs. Chalmers have any suspicions who might be responsible? How long ago did it occur? The names of her sister's friends. And when he was done he crossed his legs and glanced quickly around the room. "That's all I need to know right now. But I do want to advise you that the odds of turning up something new and revealing are pretty slim."

"I understand," said Mrs. Chalmers, with an odd catch in her voice; and that, combined with an almost unconscious nod of her head seemed to express some inner approval of Steve. She continued, "I want you to do everything possible to find those responsible. If it is so much as an insignificant lead, I want it followed until you are sure it means nothing. Is that clearly understood?"

"I understand. But are you sure you understand what such a request means in terms of manpower, and money? There is a point in any investigation where—"

She held her hands away from her body, palms up, as if to say, Do you doubt I have enough?

"All right," Steve said quietly, realizing how very deeply this matriarch must be feeling the desecration of her sister's grave.

Steve heard girlish giggling behind him, and noticed an immediate softening of Mrs. Chalmers's expression. A delicate smile came to her lips as she glanced past him. "Well, come in girls," she said. "I'll introduce you and then you have to go and play." She looked back to Steve: "I hope you don't mind." Before Steve could respond the two little girls who had been playing outside marched around his chair and over to their grandmother, their Cabbage Patch kids in tow.

The eldest was about eleven, Steve guessed, and looked like a child version of Mrs. Chal-

24

mers, right down to the intelligent, penetrating eyes. She brushed her chestnut-colored hair back with one delicate hand as her grandmother introduced her as Daphne. "I'm Duffy," the girl corrected her grandmother, "and this is Beans." She poked her brown-haired little sister who was crowding next to her, half hiding, half teasing Steve with a freckled-face smile. She had different features than her sister, a rounder face, and pug nose.

"Daphne," Mrs. Chalmers cautioned. "Introduce your sister to Mr. Brogan if you wish, but do it properly."

The girl shrugged her shoulders, and said, "Her real name in Penelope Ann. She's eight, and everybody calls her Beans."

"Like in jellybean?" Steve offered.

Duffy giggled. "Like in pork-and-beans. She loves to eat them."

Beans nodded her head in big floppy motions, and grinned. "It's true," she giggled. "We're a team, Duffy and Beans."

Steve smiled broadly, and said, "Well, I am pleased to meet the team, of Duffy and Beans," which sent the girls into giggles, and solicited a kind smile from Carlotta Chalmers.

"Girls." The woman's voice came from behind Steve's chair. He stood up and turned around.

And he was stunned by the beauty of the woman that faced him. She was a younger embodiment of Carlotta Chalmers, perhaps in her late twenties at most. She had the same sharp

25

intelligent blue eyes as her mother. Her long chestnut hair swept back and spilled onto her cream-colored dress. Her mouth was full and skin healthy with life. When she spoke, her voice held the same cultured timbre as Carlotta. "Girls," she said. "Go and play. Go on now."

The girls gave him a parting giggle, and ran out of the room.

Carlotta stood up. "My granddaughter, Molly Daniels, Mr. Brogan. Molly, this is Mr. Brogan."

Granddaughter! Steve was stunned. That would make Carlotta Chalmers at least seventy years old, and she didn't look a day over fifty. He wanted to think that she'd misspoken, but instinct told him that she hadn't done so.

"How do you do, Mr. Brogan," Molly said. Her tone of voice was pleasant enough, but her eyes were slightly cold to him. She touched his offered hand briefly. "I must tell you that I am totally against this—"

"I haven't told him yet, Molly."

"Oh," was all she said.

Steve assumed they were talking about the second item that Mrs. Chalmers hadn't gotten to yet. "Well, why don't you tell me about it," he said. He was having a hard time keeping his eyes off of Molly. Even with the hostility she was radiating towards him he felt a strong attraction, one he hadn't thought possible since Constance had left him.

The ladies sat down, and Steve did so, too.

26

With both pairs of blue eyes staring at him, he felt his wing-back chair had become a hot seat.

"What Carlotta wants," began Molly, "is for you to find Duffy's father. I forbid it."

Steve nodded comprehension, and noticed that she wasn't wearing a wedding ring. Now, if he could get her to stop hating him, maybe he could get somewhere. "You two will have to work this out among yourselves," said Steve.

"Molly," Mrs. Chalmers's voice was somber. "We have tried everything else. Dr. Hochner—"

"Dr. Hochner is grasping at straws. Bob can't be called her father. He's never seen her. Hochner doesn't know what he's talking about."

"But the dreams, Molly."

"She doesn't need to meet a man she's never known. I don't see how it relates to her problem, anyway."

"It's for Duffy's own good, the poor dear. And meeting her father might make a real difference. The doctor thinks so, anyway. She can't endure these fits much longer. Even you can see—"

"She'll be fine! I'll get another doctor!"

"You're thinking of yourself, Molly."

"I am thinking of the good of my little girl, who has never seen—"

A child's scream cut through both women's arguing, and brought Steve to his feet. Molly and Mrs. Chalmers brushed past him, and he followed them into the hall. He heard the sound of glass exploding as he followed the woman up the stairs and down a long hall, and into a large upstairs den. As they entered, a bulbous blue-and-white cloisonné vase, ten feet from anyone in the room, exploded, sending shards flying throughout the room, luckily hitting no one.

Little Beans was doing the screaming, jumping up and down, standing next to Duffy, who was standing stiff with her arms outstretched, her eyes open and rolled back so that the whites glistened wetly. Her tongue was sticking out of her mouth, and a bestial lowing sound issued forth.

Molly rushed to her and embraced her.

Steve stepped further into the room and heard the crunching of glass for each of his steps. The knickknacks and vases that had filled the room were almost all shattered and lay in pieces around the room. What in the hell had caused that?

Mrs. Chalmers grabbed Beans and held her, while Molly let go of Duffy and tried to talk to her: "Calm down! Calm down!"

The girl drew in her tongue, then her eyelids fluttered and Steve could see the blue pupils again. "That's my baby," Molly cooed.

Suddenly, the girl opened her eyes wide. She screamed and broke away from her mother, then threw herself into Steve's arms. "Daddy, Daddy," she screamed. "Don't let them hurt me! Please! Please! Don't let them hurt me!"

Steve grappled to get a secure hold on the girl. He hugged her tightly, felt her weight and the shuddering of her body. He smelled sweat that true terror makes, mingled with the salt of her tears. He rocked her gently, staring at her mother.

"You see, Molly," said Mrs. Chalmers, "it's getting worse. We've done everything else. Did you hear her call out for her father? Now, let's follow the doctor's advice . . . we have to, dear. Don't you see?"

Blinking back tears, Molly turned to Steve, and said, "Find her father for us. Please."

"You can count on it," said Steve.

Three

CASE TWO

Steve laid Duffy down on her bed next to a Raggedy Ann doll. He'd been holding and rocking her for five minutes. She had finally calmed down, after a fit when Steve had tried to give her to Molly. Her eyes were closed, and her sobs had diminished to snuffles.

He touched her forehead. "She's hot," he said. "It's from the tears, though. She'll be all right."

He turned from the bed, and thought it odd that he had such an audience: Mrs. Chalmers, her dogs, Motu, and two twin dwarf women crowded and watched from near the doorway. Even Duffy's mother, Molly, stood with the others, her youngest daughter in her arms. And they were staring, not unkindly, at *him,* not at little Duffy. Oh God, he really had taken over, hadn't he? But what was he supposed to do—the poor kid had been clinging to him in a death grip.

"Radinka. Radella," commanded Mrs. Chalmers, and without another word the little twin women left the room. "Motu," she said, and the big Samoan walked past Steve, and stood near the bed, obviously to monitor little Duffy.

Steve wondered how the hell they knew what she wanted them to do. It must be old drill when Duffy had a seizure.

Beans twisted in Molly's arms, and asked, "Mommy, can I stay with Duffy? Please?"

"Sure, honey. But be very quiet, understand?"

Beans nodded her head, and Molly let her down. She ran to Steve, gave him a mournful look to show that she was sad about Duffy, then pulled up a little rocking chair and sat down in it, watching her sister with firm determination as if her presence alone would make her well.

"Mr. Brogan," said Mrs. Chalmers; she turned, the dogs preceding her, and left.

Now *I'm* doing it, thought Steve. He followed Mrs. Chalmers down the long second-floor hall, Molly walking silently beside him. At the stairs, Mrs. Chalmers stopped and extended her hand to Steve. "I'll leave you with Molly for whatever information you may need to find Duffy's father. I'll expect to hear from you soon. Good day."

"Good day, Mrs. Chalmers," said Steve, and followed Molly down the stairs and into the sitting room. What luck, he thought. It was just what he wanted anyway—to be alone with Molly. Since the minute he had seen her he'd been interested. He thought that she had to be single. She's not wearing a wedding band, and

31

she didn't mention her husband—for some reason, women always seemed to mention their husbands, if they had one. A boyfriend, though: she might have a boyfriend.

They seated themselves, as before, and Steve saw Molly take a deep breath, and he realized that whatever she was about to tell him was very traumatic to her.

He asked the bare minimum of questions about Daphne's father.

She answered each of the questions softly, her hands neatly in her lap, playing absently with the rings on her fingers. Duffy's father's name was John Chadwick. She knew that he would be forty, now, because he was exactly ten years older than herself. She had seen him twelve years ago, six months before Duffy was born.

Molly stopped here, and looked intently at Steve. "I was in love with him," she said. "We were to be married. The last reaction I expected from him, when I told about the baby was for him to deny that the child was his. It had to be his, if you understand what I mean. He was the only . . . only person."

Steve nodded in sympathy. The guy probably got cold feet about the marriage, and used the baby as an excuse. "So, that was the last time you saw him, then?"

"Yes. He went back to Atlanta, I heard. If it weren't for Duffy, I'd never want to see him again."

"I can't say that I blame you, Miss Daniels."

"It's Molly," she said.

"Okay, Molly. I'm Steve."

She nodded, then continued: "This seizure is the worst Duffy has ever had. We've tried everything—the doctors find nothing physically wrong with her, so we're with a shrink, now—he says something about an unresolved conflict dealing with her father, or, lack of father, I should say. Supposedly, by seeing her father this conflict will resolve itself. I doubt it, myself, but after today's seizure, I'm willing to try anything. John was so cold about my pregnancy, I doubt if he will help even if we find him. I never understood why he was so quick to call me a slut, and deny his own child. He was very religious—" She snorted in irony. "He probably couldn't face his born-again friends.

"All I care about now is Duffy. Please find her father, Steve."

Steve said that he would, and then asked several more questions about John Chadwick. She told him that his middle name was Loyal, and that he had been in the navy and served off the coast of Nam, the Gulf of Tonkin. He'd served on a carrier, she didn't know which one. He was an officer. "A flyer?" Steve asked, and she said "No." She said that the last she knew, his parents lived in Ellenwood, Georgia.

Finished, Steve rose to go.

She said she would walk him to his car. He wanted to ask her out right now, but she was a client. He'd have to wait until he had finished

33

up both cases, then perhaps things would work out . . . he hadn't really met anyone he liked since Constance had left him. Christ, the house had seemed so lonely since then.

As they left the porch and reached his car, a black Cadillac Seville drove up, and a short, dark-haired man got out. "It's Thom," said Molly with a lover's lilt in her voice that cut Steve to the quick.

"Your husband?" Steve asked.

"No. My boyfriend."

Crap, he thought. He knew it looked too good to be true.

What's more, Steve hated the guy on sight. He had cold, ink blue eyes, and when Steve shook his hand it was soft and dry. With his dark suit, he reminded Steve of a mortician. A guy like that didn't go with Molly at all. What the hell could she see in him? He looked like a stiff himself.

"I better be going," said Steve. "Nice to meet you," he nodded toward Thom, then got in the car.

"What's he doing here?" Steve heard Thom ask Molly.

Molly's voice got wet: "There's something we have to talk about, Thom. Let's go inside."

Steve started the car as they walked toward the house.

I hope he can't handle it, thought Steve. I hope she tells him, and he can't handle it at all.

* * *

Steve pulled into a Seven-Eleven, and checked his watch. It was almost five-thirty, that would make it about eight-thirty back East. He still had time to make the call and visit the cemetery.

He bought a cup of coffee, and laced it with non-dairy creamer and sugar, then returned to his car. Using his car phone he called Atlanta information and got three telephone numbers for Ellenwood, Georgia—all of them Chadwicks, but none of them for John Loyal Chadwick, Duffy's father. But if luck were with him, one of the three would be Chadwick's parents, and Steve could take it from there.

He went over in his mind the information that Molly had given him about Chadwick, decided what his story would be, then made his call. The first didn't work out, but on the second a young-sounding woman answered, "Hello."

"Yes, hi. I'm not sure I have the right number. I'm looking for an old navy buddy, John Chadwick; his middle name's Loyal—served together in Nam. We're having a reunion . . ."

"Oh, yes," she said. "That's my brother."

"Great. Listen, do you have his telephone number and address? I'd like to give him a call. And I've got the information on the reunion I want to send him."

"Yes. Just a minute." She was back shortly, and Steve wrote down the information in his pocket notebook.

"Thank you, very much," he said. "What's your name?"

"Pam," she said.

"Great, Pam. Listen, what the heck is John doing out in California? Movie star or something?"

She laughed. "No, no. He sells insurance."

"You're kidding?"

"That's what he does."

"What company is he working for?"

"Metropolitan."

"And that's in Redondo Beach, where he lives?"

"Yes, that's right."

"Do you have the number there, just in case I can't get him at home?"

"Sure," she said, and gave him the number.

"Thanks, Pam. And did he get married?"

"Yes. Finally. We thought he'd never get married."

"Any kids?"

"No."

"Oh, well. Thanks for your help, Pam."

"Wait a minute? I didn't get your name."

"John'll remember me as Angel—my nickname's Angel. Thanks again," he said, and hung up.

He wrote down Pam's name, and that he'd told her the fictitious nickname Angel, in case he had to call her back.

For a moment a small feeling of guilt washed over him. One of the things that he had to get used to when he got into this business was the necessity of misrepresenting himself. It helped to be a good actor in this job, and after so many years, he could pull a routine off pretty well. But he still didn't like the way he felt afterwards.

Now, he had all the information he needed, and all Pam knew about him, was that he was supposed to be a navy buddy of her brother, and that his supposed nickname was Angel.

As for Steve, he knew that the man Molly wanted lived about thirty-five miles away from her. Wouldn't that be a shock to her? Sounded like he was pretty well settled down, too.

Steve closed the notebook, and started the car. It was close to dusk, but he could still make the cemetery. He knew there was a caretaker on premises— Chatsworth Cemetery was where he had buried George Flynn, one of Steve's agents who had died in the Balatta Sting. The caretaker had been there to lead the procession of cars to the grave site.

As he pulled up to the closed wrought-iron gates, memories fought to rise in Steve's mind, but he shoved them down. He was working now, and feelings and thoughts about his old friend would have to wait. Still, a sadness hung about him as he got out of his car and glanced at the padlocked chain coiled around the two sections of gate like a long, black snake. Man, this guy didn't want anybody getting in.

In the light of the dusk, Steve searched for a buzzer button on the old brick wall. It had probably been years since anyone had come after closing, but Steve had a good reason—whoever had violated Mary Hull's grave, had come at night; and he wanted to see what they saw, smell what they smelled, get into their frame of mind, and think what they thought—if possible, that is.

He brushed aside one last patch of ivy, and found a plastic ivory-colored button and pressed it. He wasn't even sure if it worked, but he kept pressing it until he finally heard the engine of a car purring along from the other side of the gate. It was only then that he let up on the buzzer, and that the premonition struck him cold like a frozen rod through the center of his brain—

This wasn't a simple case at all; this one was gonna be a bitch.

Steve moved to the gate and stood before the snakelike chain, and waited for the caretaker to let him in.

Four

DWIGHT KLEIBER

In the beginning Dwight Kleiber had been skeptical of Eva's powers, but his attraction for her was strong enough, and her wealth was vast enough, to draw him to her side, and he became her attorney.

His colleagues thought him crazy, giving up his Beverly Hills law practice to handle a single client in the small, mountain community of Hennington, just outside of Los Angeles County. But they could not have known, nor would they ever know, the extent of power and wealth his decision had provided for him in just five short years.

Of course, there had been sacrifices, thought Kleiber, as he brushed a few strands of brown hair over his balding pate, and picked up his oxblood leather briefcase. That's what his wife, Anna, hadn't understood, and why she had tried to escape.

Thank God Eva hadn't held Anna's ingratitude against him. Or, had she? Is that what she wanted to see him about today?

Kleiber shuddered involuntarily at the thought. Eva's justice was not always swift, but it was inevitable, and very unpleasant. No, he decided. He was too important to her for one thing, and for another, it hadn't been his fault. *Anna* had been the one unwilling to sacrifice, not he.

He shook off the disturbing feelings and left his office, stepping out into the dusky glow of close of day. Traffic was light down Buford Street, the main street running through the center of Hennington. He slipped behind the wheel of his black Cadillac, started up, and drove ten minutes out of town. He turned off at a pasture road and drove up it for a quarter mile, and then branched off onto a well-worn dirt road, that was swallowed by a forest of tall pines.

He flicked on his lights when he reached the trees. Although it was not night, the tall pines blocked out most of the ebbing light. His headlight beams caught the dusty road and the scaly bark of the trees. He cracked his window and whiffed the pungent, clean smell of the pines. He loved that smell; and the sound of the winds soughing through the evergreens.

Soon, the trees fell away into an open pasture that ran up against the mountains, where more trees took riotous growth up the steep slopes. Kleiber stopped the car, and waited impatiently for the signal. There! Two headlights flashed on and off twice. It was about time. In the dusk he could barely make out the shape of the jeep. He flicked his lights on-off, on-off, then kept them off. The jeep pulled out from the far side of the trees, and carried four armed men, dressed in grey cowled robes, toward him.

The jeep curved around as it approached and came up behind him. Kleiber lowered the window completely. "You sure took your time getting down here," he said. "I'm in a hurry. Pull back your cowl."

It was Jenson, a rookie policeman from town, who owed his job to Eva. "Sorry, Mr. Kleiber."

"Next time, you better come flying down like a bat out of hell! You hear me?!"

"Yes sir."

"All right. Our Lady, where is she?"

"She's walking, sir."

"Okay. Escort me to the parking area. You aren't too new to know where that is, are you?"

"No sir."

Kleiber followed the jeep, that *was* now moving like a bat out of hell toward the far side of the pasture. At the time of the Gatherings, fully a third of this huge pasture was filled with the cars of the Faithful.

He parked and left the security force without a word. Instead of heading toward the Caverns, whose small opening was hidden from view by a labyrinth of granite stone and trees, he entered a small copse of pines that shielded the pasture from a downward-sloping meadow where Eva took her ritual dusk-time walk.

He paused for a moment, as he always did before entering Eva's presence, to gain composure and organize his thoughts. Once again the paranoia crept in—*She's going to punish me for Anna's doings,* his mind said. He struggled with the thought for a moment more, then subdued it. He was being ridiculous. Eva often sent for him. He was her attorney, and her right arm in the Order. There were big events in the offing, but they had discussed those plans yesterday. He cleared his mind as best he could, and followed the path out onto the upper edge of the meadow.

The clearing ran down and away from him in ankle-high summer grass and multicolored flowers. The lower edge of the meadow gave onto a distant vista of the flatlands, bathed in the fiery red turmoil of the sun's dying rays.

Kleiber searched the meadow and felt the little gaff in his heart that he always did when first coming into Lady Eva's presence. He spotted her walking near the center of the meadow, next to a chest-high granite boulder that always seemed to him as if it had been dumped there as an afterthought by the creative gods of the universe.

Her back was to him, but he sensed that she knew of his presence. She was dressed in a long black robe of heavy cotton. Her long silky black hair flowed down to her ankles. Hundreds of ravens and crows waddled behind her step, flowing behind her like a river of ink. Kleiber felt the sexual yearning for her, that he discovered most people, both men and woman, also felt. She was special. He felt that he knew how one of the Apostles of Jesus must have felt, being in the presence of such a powerful, and wondrous person. But unlike Jesus, what dark wonders this woman commanded.

"Come!" she said, without turning her head.

Kleiber started down the hill, and watched as Lady Eva raised both arms from her sides, and the black birds rose up like a dark cloud, then flew away into the gathering night.

As he approached her he looked up to his left and then right to the forest, trying to spot Cutter and Radd, her bodyguards. To his surprise, they were not there, nor was Sloat, her son.

"My Lady, is it wise to be so unguarded?"

She whirled around and faced him. Her beautiful face was twisted into a fearsome mask. Her blue, blue eyes, went wild for a moment; her lips curled up in lupine anger. "Would you not defend me, my dear Dwight?! Die for me?!"

Shapeless fear rose in him. His knees felt weak. He bowed his head. "I obey your every word, My Lady."

She said nothing for a moment. He kept his eyes fixed at the hem of her long dress. He tried to figure out why she should be angry about an appropriate question. Although the mountain was secure, it was always foolish to take unnecessary risks. Besides, she was never without Cutter or Radd, unless she was in the Caverns.

He heard her give a forgiving sigh. She spoke softly to him now. "Your concern that I blame you for your wife's treachery is why I am angry with you, Dwight."

Dwight still did not look up. He felt a mild shock. He knew that to some sporadic degree she was telepathic. Unfortunately for him, she had picked up his fears. And they had angered her.

She touched his face. His erection rose full and hard now. It hurt. She lifted his chin and stared into his eyes. He came in his pants. "If I blamed you, Dwight," she said, "would you not be suffering this minute?"

"Yes," he answered judiciously, knowing that in reality, if it served her purpose, Eva could wait until hell froze over to mete out her punishment. She was a gifted strategist.

"Then perhaps you have some other reason for feeling this way. Perhaps, you are not faithful enough to make the sacrifice, as dear Anna was not faithful enough? Is that it, my dear Dwight?"

"My God, no, Eva!" Nothing could mute the instantaneous fear in his voice.

She stared at him, and looking into her eyes he knew first hand the embodiment of evil within her. It writhed deep in those blue eyes like a nest of black snakes. How could he love and fear one woman so much, at one time? "I *want* to make the sacrifice, Eva! I *want* to! You must know that!"

She took her hand from his face, and laughed, as if the interchange had all been for her amusement. "Yes, yes. I know that," she said. "I know that very well. You are too much in love with me, and too much in love with the power that serving me gives you, not to make the sacrifice." She turned from him, and began a stroll down the meadow. "Come walk with me. Talk with me. We have more business to discuss. I have good news, for us both."

Kleiber followed, relieved that Eva had returned to her normal temperament. She *enjoyed* that! he thought, to the same degree that I hated it!

Eva stopped and turned around, and smiled as if the most wondrous news was about to leave her lips. "Dwight, I have made a sacrifice . . ." She reached in the folds of her robe and pulled forth the brace of three sacred coins that she wore as a necklace . . . "And Satan has told me that the time of The Virgin is nearly here. The time of the Convergence is at hand."

Dwight was staring at the brace so hard that he scarcely heard her words. The center coin was missing! In the Order, that meant the coming of The Virgin . . . she'd just said that!

"My Lady . . ."

"The coin was employed, per my bidding . . ."

"But, My Lady, the *Das Fayden* is needed."

He stared at her incredulously. "Do you have it?"

"No," she said, "but that book will be found soon. Timothy has heard reliable rumors that it has been unearthed. He is tracing its where-abouts, now. Have faith. It has been revealed to me that the Time of the Virgin is at hand. And it will coincide with the Great Gathering of The Order."

Kleiber's mind was reeling. What Eva was talking about was on par with the second coming of Christ. And he, Dwight Kleiber, would be there! At Eva's right hand!

The Great Gathering was to occur in a few weeks—the leaders of the Faithful from all over the country would come to pay their respect and homage to Lady Eva, to unify under her absolute control. No doubt, some of the more ungrateful members were the reason that Sloat, Eva's son, was not here. He had probably gone with Cutter and Radd to settle matters.

"And the Virgin?" asked Kleiber.

"All in good time," said Eva. She nodded back toward the Caverns. "Another sacrifice must be made, Dwight. I give you that honor."

"Thank you."

"You are sure that you have no hesitation?" she asked in a toying tone of voice. "After all, he is, what . . . only three months old, isn't he?"

Kleiber cleared his throat. "About that," he said, and thought of how hard it had been for

Anna and him to conceive a child. So much work, and sweat, and worry, in what should be a very natural event. No wonder Anna had run when Lady Eva had demanded the sacrifice. Anna had been six months pregnant at the time, and active in the Order, a high priestess; very willing to see the children of other women sacrificed, but not so willing with her own child. Poor Anna. In a way, Kleiber could have foretold that Eva would ask it of them—he and Anna were Eva's right hands, and Eva *had* to test their loyalty. The only difference was that he had understood that, and agreed; Anna had not.

When Eva caught Anna, she had Dr. Sturgeon amputate both her legs, then put her in the ampward of the brooding chambers in the Caverns. The child, a son, had been born, and Anna was allowed to nurse it until it was time for the sacrifice. That time was very near, now.

"It's a great honor, My Lady," said Kleiber. "To be allowed to sacrifice for your glory."

She had led him back up to a granite boulder. "I am glad you feel that way, my Dwight," she said, bending down and picking up a small bundle of black silk. She handed it to him. It felt light, and fragile. "Open it," she said.

He pushed back the folds, and stared. He was holding two withered, old hands. They were small, woman's hands.

"Who called me into the Order, Dwight?"

He looked up at her from the hands. "Why . . . Jobina, of course. The great Jobina . . ."

Lady Eva's eyes flashed excitedly. She said, "And it was Jobina who found the Caverns for me, was it not?"

"Yes."

"And great things, like the Caverns, need great sacrifice, is that not correct, my Dwight?"

"Yes, My Lady."

"So it was Jobina's blood that I used to anoint the walls of the Cavern, though I loved her dearly."

"Really?" Dwight felt shock. Suddenly, the light withered old hands seemed very heavy. He looked at them, then up at Eva, the dawning of understanding coming over his face. "These . . . these are . . ."

"True Hands of Glory. Jobina's hands. I had Sloat fetch them for me recently."

"This is truly an honor."

"Yes, it is, isn't it, my Dwight? Now go to the Caverns and prepare—the sacrifice is within two days."

Dwight turned to go, but she stopped him and let him look deep into her eyes. His peripheral vision caught the red flames of the sun making a corona in her hair, like the flames of hell.

"Dwight," she said, in a serious tone so that he would know that she was not toying with him. "Don't think that I send you lightly to sacrifice your son. I sacrificed mine twenty-five years ago when he was just a boy of five. It hurt at the time. The evisceration was the worst part.

"But later that night, when Jobina first hailed me Lady Eva, Queen of the Coven of the Dark Dream, there was a knock on the door, and there stood my little boy, a red seam up his belly—you see, Satan was merciful to His faithful—he sent Sloat back from the dead, to me, to grow up, and be at my side—to aid me in fulfilling the Dark Dream.

"So, in truth, I do understand. But most likely you will not be as lucky as I." She stopped abruptly and smiled maternally at him. "What I've told you about Sloat is the truth, my Dwight."

Kleiber stood rigid, thinking of Sloat, letting what Eva said sink in. He felt light-headed as he thought of what he knew about Sloat, and about Cutter and Radd, and about Eva's powers. He looked up and said to her: "I know it is the truth, My Lady." He clutched the silk bundle containing Jobina's hands to his chest, and said more formally, according to custom, "Thou art truly a dark wonder, My Lady." He bowed, turned, and left her to the dark of night.

Five

THE GIRLS

Penny heard the car start up, ran and climbed up on the cushioned window seat to peek down at the drive. Duffy moaned behind her and Penny quickly looked back to see if she was all right.

Duffy seemed okay. She was scrunched up in her brass bed, hugging her yellow-haired Cabbage Patch Kid, that she had named Kathleen. Suzette, Penny's carrot-haired Cabbage Patch Kid, lay by Duffy's side where Penny had put her to protect Duffy. Penny wasn't going to let anything happen to her sister, 'cause she *loved* her; she wasn't going to leave her either. Just 'cause Grandma and Mommy had come in and said Duffy was okay—just sleeping, didn't mean it was so. Penny knew better: one time she'd left her daddy just sleeping, and the next morning, he was just gone. Mommy said she and Daddy weren't going to live together anymore. If she had been there when Daddy had waked up she could have stopped him from leaving—it had been her fault that Daddy left, and she knew it! She wasn't leaving Duffy alone until Duffy woke up, and she knew Duffy was okay.

Penny turned back to the window and brushed the white gauzy curtain aside. Thom's car was pulling away, and she was glad. She didn't like him at all—neither did Duffy.

"What are you looking at Penny-Peanut?"

Penny whipped around. "Duffy!" She ran to her sister and hugged and kissed her.

Duffy struggled to sit up, and asked, "What were you looking at?"

"Thom-the-Bomb. He just drove off."

"Good. What about the other man? He's nice."

Penny giggled. "You called him 'Daddy,' Duffy. You called him 'Daddy.' And he picked you up and he hugged you tight. He's the one who put you in bed. Do you remember?"

"I don't remember anything, Penny-Peanut, except we were playing. Did I break things again? Did I?"

"Mommy said it's not your fault, 'member?"

"But I did, didn't I?"

"Mom said it's not your *fault,* Duffy. It's part of when you're sick. So don't be so sad. Please."

Duffy straightened up and leaned back against a pillow. "Okay," she said, but Penny could tell it still bothered her.

"What's his name?" asked Duffy, and Penny saw a picture of the nice man appear in her mind, the way pictures did sometimes when Duffy thought about things.

"Mr. Broken," said Penny. "I think that's what Grandma Lottie said. He left a long time ago." And Duffy started laughing.

"Mr. Brogan. That was it. Not Broken."

"Oh."

"He's rad."

That meant great, Penny knew. She thought he was rad, too. And she wished he had held her in his arms the way he'd held Duffy, when she was sick.

"I'm in love with him," said Duffy.

"I love him, too," said Penny because if Duffy did, so did she.

"No. Not like I love him." Duffy gave her what Mom called *The Look,* scrunching up her face and staring at her with slit eyes. "No, Penny-Peanut. I'm going to marry him."

"So am I, Duffy."

"No, you're not. He can only marry one of us."

"Why?"

"Because. Besides you're not old enough. I'll be twelve next month."

It didn't sound fair. "You called him Daddy," said Penny. "Maybe he'll marry Mommy. I wish he would, and Thom-the-Bomb would disappear."

"No. He's gonna marry me." Duffy swept the

covers aside and sat on the side of the bed. "You know what I'm gonna do, Penny-Peanut?"

Penny shook her head.

"I'm gonna borrow Mommy's book. It tells how to do all kinds of things. It tells how to get a man to love you."

Penny took a deep breath and stared at Duffy with big pop-eyes. "You better not. Mommy said never touch her books. You know that."

"We won't tell her," said Duffy, including Penny in the adventure, "and we'll put it back after we use it. She won't miss it, anyway. I don't think she looks at it anymore."

"Okay," said Penny.

"Let's go get it, now."

Penny watched Duffy slide out of bed. "Duffy, maybe you shouldn't get out . . ."

"I'm fine," said Duffy, heading for the door. "Come on."

Penny followed her down the hall to Mommy's room, wishing she wouldn't walk so fast. Maybe Mommy was in her room. The door was open. Duffy whisked in, and Penny followed her, past the antique cherrywood chest of drawers with the swivel mirror on top, and the four-poster king-sized bed, that she and Duffy loved to bounce on, and sometimes on rainy nights, crawl into, under the warm down covers and sleep with Mommy.

Duffy scooted directly into Mommy's walk-in closet, down the alley formed by the dresses on either side, while Penny stopped to pet Mr.

Shiny, the brass penguin stop, holding the closet door open.

"Here it is," said Duffy. "Turn on the light, Beans."

Penny reached up and pushed the switch up. "You better hurry, Duffy. Mommy might come."

Duffy knelt down besides a large brass-bound trunk, popped the catches and opened the lid. Beans padded forward and peaked inside—nothing but books. Old books.

Duffy picked up a worn leather one, held it up. "This is it," she said. She put the book down, closed the lid and fastened the catches, then Beans turned off the light, and they scuttled as fast as they could back to Duffy's room.

Duffy hid the book under her bed.

"I want to see," said Beans.

"No. Later. Mommy's coming."

A picture of Mommy walking up the stairs suddenly filled Beans's head—Duffy was sensing it, and something more—Beans could feel what Mommy was feeling—sad—and now Beans felt sad too.

"She'll be okay," said Duffy. "She's going to ask us if we want to sleep with her tonight. She's going to read us a story—she doesn't know which one yet."

The picture of Mommy disappeared. "How do you do that?" asked Beans.

"I'm not supposed to. Sometimes, it just happens. *Sh.* Here comes Mommy."

Molly paused on the stairs, her hand lightly touching the mahogany banister. She surrendered to the feeling of sadness that had been brewing all day, letting it fill her so that she could get rid of it. Duffy's seizure had scared her the most, of course. (She was all right, now, thank goodness.) But overall it hadn't been an easy day at all: having to tell a complete stranger, that Steve Brogan, that she was an unwed mother, and then repeating it to Thom—she wasn't sure how he would take it, he was so conservative, but he had taken it well, although he did look a little upset when she explained that Steve Brogan was a detective, who was going to find Duffy's father. Jealousy, she guessed. Or, was he jealous of Steve Brogan?

She could tell Brogan had an interest in her. The way he had looked at her. But she knew about him. She had read the papers about the Balatta Sting, and how he had put his wife and children's lives in danger, though she thought that information inconsistent with his actions today. He'd held Duffy with such tender affection, his concern so obvious and unaffected. The girls had warmed to him immediately, too. Why couldn't they like Thom that way? she wondered.

Thom cared, she knew. He expressed it differently, that was all. He had listened keenly when she had told him that Duffy had a bad seizure, and said that he had faith she would be well soon. She knew that he would ask her to marry him soon, they'd talked about it a little. But before he even asked she would have to tell him the history of her family, it was only fair. And how he reacted to that would tell her whether she could marry him or not.

Grandma Lottie didn't like him much, but Molly had to make her own choices now. Use her head a little. John Chadwick had charmed her and left her pregnant. Her marriage to Tim Daniels some four years later lasted two years, ending with Tim going off to Africa to study baboons, or gorillas or some other damn thing. She knew she wasn't a stupid woman, she'd just made bad choices, and she wasn't going to repeat the mistake again. Yes, Thom was conservative with his emotions, but he was stable. And he had told her he loved her. She knew that he wasn't the kind to leave a woman flat, or ignore a commitment by flying off to some far corner of the earth. The real question was did she love him? Grandma Lottie had asked that one. And she'd said very flippantly, "I'm not sure I know what real love is," and let it go at that. Maybe there were things more important than deep love in a relationship, she thought. After all, how many people are truly in love with their spouses after the first few years of marriage? She didn't know for sure, but she did know a lot of unhappily married people, that was for sure.

The real kicker for the day of course was Duffy's seizure. And of course Grandma Lottie's intimation that Molly was protesting having Steve Brogan find Duffy's father—for reasons of pride—a nasty thing to say. And not true. It was just that she didn't believe what Dr. Hochner had said. She didn't see what good bringing John Chadwick into this would do. Duffy didn't know her father, and he didn't know her. The bastard had completely refused to acknowledge his responsibility at all. He wouldn't even talk to Molly after she had told him she was pregnant—had called her a slut. How could he say that—all his Christian beliefs suddenly reared their head. They weren't so evident when he was talking her into making love with him.

She shook her head as if breaking a spell, and started up the stairs. The sadness still prevailed, but she knew a good cure for that—the girls loved to sleep with her, and tonight it was their mom that needed the company; she could read to them, but what book? Maybe *Where the Wild Things Are,* she loved that story herself.

She rapped lightly on the door, then opened it. There Duffy was, sitting right up on her bed, Beans beside her. Mischievous grins lit up their faces so much, it was impossible to tell that something had been wrong just hours before.

"And what have you two been up to?" she asked, feeling happy at the sight of the girls.

"Sister stuff, Mom," answered Duffy.

Beans giggled. "Sister stuff, Mommy. Mommy, can we sleep with you tonight?"

"Do you have a sleep-with-Mommy ticket?"

Beans held up imaginary tickets. "I have two," she said.

"Okay." She walked over and sat down close to Duffy. "You doing okay, now?"

"Yes, Mom." Duffy looked down slyly at her hands. "Mom, is Mr. Brogan coming back soon?"

"I don't know if he'll be back at all."

"Duffy loves him, Mommy," piped in Beans.

"Shut up Penny-Peanut," said Duffy, and before Molly could reprimand her, she asked, "Do you like him, Mommy?"

"Steve Brogan?"

"Yes."

"Well, I guess I do. He's a stranger; it's hard to tell from only one encounter."

Duffy wrinkled up her nose, and clutched her doll. "Sometimes you can like someone you just meet a lot more than someone you've known a long time."

"Like Mr. Broken," said Beans, causing Molly to laugh.

"Brogan, dear," said Molly.

"I already told her, Mom," said Duffy.

"We like him a lot more than Thom-the-Bomb," said Beans.

"I told you never to call him that, Penelope!" Molly stared hard at Beans to make sure she got the message. "Do you understand?"

Beans stuck out her lower lip and started to cry.

Molly felt bad immediately. It had been a hard

day for Beans, too, she realized. She was crazy about Duffy, and worried sick about her too.

Molly decided to drop the subject of Thom; she would try later to make them understand that Thom liked them and wanted them to like him. For now, she would try to get the waterworks turned off.

She softened her tone a little and said, "Can't take a sleep-with-Mommy ticket from a little girl who's crying, y'know." Beans nodded her head a little, and began to dry up. "Okay, why don't you girls get into your pj's and I'll meet you in my room. Okay?"

"Okay," said Duffy.

Beans nodded her head, but said nothing.

Molly kissed them both and started for the door. She turned and looked at them. They were staring at her like two little pixies. "What?" asked Molly

"We love you, Mommy," they both said in unison.

Tears welled up in Molly's eyes. "I love you, too," she said.

Duffy pursed her lips, and tugging absently at her doll's hair, said: "Mommy, you know how I know things sometimes, and I don't know how I know them or what they mean?"

"Yes, dear." Molly felt a cold shiver down her spine—Duffy's sporadic psychic abilities had proved less than amusing a number of times.

Molly took a shallow breath.

Duffy's eyes were like dull bits of green glass.

Her speech was slow and syrupy. "I know that you should ask Mr. Brogan if what they said about him is true. He hasn't told anyone the truth, but he'll tell you. He protected them, Mommy—and he'll protect you, too."

Six

GRAVESIDE CHAT

The caretaker, caught in the headlights of Steve's car, wasn't what he had expected. Instead of the old, crotchety, half-tanked curmudgeon of the movies, he found himself face to face with a man in his mid-thirties with corn-colored hair and washed blue eyes. He was dressed in a tailored pair of trousers and white dress shirt and tie.

"We're closed," said the man in a high voice, "but, I guess you would know that, or you wouldn't have rung the bell."

"Yes. I'm investigating the Mary Hull grave desecration, and I'd like to get a look at the crime scene at night; and ask a few questions if that'd be all right?"

"That Cadillac doesn't look much like a police car," said the caretaker. He said it conversationally, Steve noted, not accusing, yet requiring an answer. The man's no fool, thought Steve.

"I'm retained by the Chalmers family," Steve said, pulling identification from the inside of his coat. He angled the leather badge case near the iron bars so that the caretaker could see it in the headlight beams. "I've got a car phone if you'd like to call and verify."

The caretaker leaned forward, studied the identification card intently, then stood erect with a chagrined look on his face. "You . . . you're Steve Brogan, *the* Steve Brogan—from the scandal, that government dope thing?" He stuck his hand through the bars. "It's an honor to meet you."

"Thank you," said Steve. Inwardly, he groaned. He'd never had gotten used to the way some people reacted to him after that year of unwanted media publicity. Even a year and a half of lying low hadn't killed the case or his part in it, in some people's minds. Still, it appeared he could use it to high advantage this time. He shook the offered hand and said, "The paper kinda blew my contribution to the case out of proportion . . ."

"I'm Ted Neal," he said quickly, as if he couldn't wait to get Steve inside the gates. "I'm the caretaker here." He pulled a ring of keys from his pocket, and began unlocking the chains. "I'll still have to call Mrs. Chalmers. I hope you understand."

Good man, thought Steve. "That would be

best." God, the guy's actually nervous, like I was Jack Nicholson, or somebody.

The night had full sway now, and Steve's headlights caught tombstones like grey-white ghosts, as he followed Ted Neal's Honda Civic up a curving, tree-lined road to a group of Spanish Style buildings.

"This is the office," said Neal, pointing to the flat building. "And that's the chapel there. The residence is around back."

Steve waited in the outer office, while the caretaker called Mrs. Chalmers. The door to the building opened and an attractive woman dressed in jeans and a pink blouse walked in. Late twenties Steve guessed.

"Ted," she called out, and then said "oh," at the sight of Steve. Steve thought that somehow she didn't really look surprised.

He introduced himself and told her that Ted was in his office making a telephone call.

"I'm Dorothy Neal," she said. "Pleased to meet you." She looked down demurely, then said, "Actually, Ted called me on the intercom first. We don't get many celebrities here."

Steve felt awkward. "I really never know what to say when people call me that. It was a highly publicized case. I'm an everyday person, believe me."

"Nice to meet you."

Ted came out of his office. "Mrs. Chalmers said to thank you for getting right on the case, Mr. Brogan.

"You've met Dottie?"

"Yes."

"She'll be going with us. She was actually the one who called the police and saw everything. I was studying for exams. We'll take a truck."

Steve retrieved a flashlight out of his trunk and slid into the pickup truck, Dorothy Neal tucked neatly between him and her husband.

A five-minute drive later and Steve and the Neals were standing in front of the Chalmers family plot.

Steve did not like the feeling of being in a cemetery at night. Superstitious—no, just a natural uneasiness around thousands of "dearly departed" was all.

"It was there," said Dorothy Neal, pointing with the beam of her flashlight. Steve directed his beam on the same area. "That's where the body was laid out," she continued. "The dirt was piled over there. The casket over there."

"How did you discover something was wrong, Mrs. Neal?"

"Mickey started barking and wouldn't stop. Ted told me to take him for a walk, which usually shuts her up. But when I got outside Mickey took off deep into the cemetery. I didn't want to disturb Ted, so I got my keys, and went after her in the car. I thought maybe some kids had gotten in. Usually, when they see the headlights they get out. But I was worried because Mickey was a German shepherd . . ."

"Was?"

Mrs. Neal directed her flashlight beam to a headstone with a cross on top; her voice cracked slightly when she said, "You can still see the stains. The bastards killed Mickey and cut her open and draped her over the headstone."

In the dark, Steve couldn't tell for sure, but he thought that Mrs. Neal was crying softly. "I know this is hard," he said, "but did you see who did it?"

"Yes. I saw shadows. The moon was full that night and I saw what I saw—"

"Dottie!" said Ted Neal, the warning in his voice vehement.

"I'm going to tell, this time, Ted! I'm tired of keeping it in! Besides, he isn't a policeman, Ted!"

"He'll think you're crazy!"

"No, he won't," said Steve. "There's nothing about Mrs. Neal that's crazy. And she's right— I'm not a cop. Have a little faith. It might be something that's important."

"It's crazy sounding," insisted Ted, his tone telling Steve that he'd calmed down a bit.

"Tell me," Steve said. He guided the woman over near the tombstone stained with her dog's blood, "and maybe we can find out who did this terrible thing." The beam of his light glinted dully off something lying on top of the tombstone. "Wait a minute," said Steve. He picked up a half-dollar sized medallion, placed it in his palm and played his light on it fully.

"It's a medal of some kind," said Mrs. Neal. "And that's a pentagram in the center—that's a devil's amulet maybe."

"Some occult thing," offered Ted.

Steve just stared at it. It had a feel to it that he couldn't explain—he didn't like having it in his hand—it felt . . . well, it felt . . . *wrong* was the word that came to mind, that and *dirty*. And it was the strangest design he had seen: a large pentagram with a crescent moon and a star inside the border of the pentagram. The star inside the large pentagram had its top point one hundred and eighty degrees opposite that of the outside top point.

"When was the last time you were out here?" he asked them both.

"To stop and look, it's been a long time. Maybe two weeks," said the caretaker, and Mrs. Neal agreed. "We would have noticed that for sure, anyway."

"I'm going to keep this for right now," said Steve. "It might help me." He slipped it into his pocket, and it even seemed to weigh on his mind, even in there.

"Sure thing," said Mr. Neal. "Anything that might help."

"Mrs. Neal, what is it that you were going to tell me that was going to sound crazy?"

The caretaker put his arm around his wife, and said in a comforting tone, "Go on, honey. Maybe he can find out what you really saw."

"I saw it!"

"Just tell me, Mrs. Neal. Please."

"I saw them running away—the shadows, three of them—only they weren't really running, they were loping sort of. You know what I mean?"

"I understand loping, yes," said Steve. "Then what happened?"

She hesitated, then said, "I saw it that way, and I'm gonna tell it that way—Devil take the hindmost: they ran and I chased them up the hill—I was so mad, I didn't even think that they might hurt me. I saw them reach the wall. Jump up on it . . . and then," she raised her hand in the darkness blotting out some stars, "I swear . . . I saw them grow wings and fly into the sky," she said quickly. "I know it sounds loony-toons, but I saw it, I swear."

"And you told the police what?" asked Steve, gaining a little thinking time with the question.

"That I saw men going over the wall, that's all."

"I can see why you left out the flying part."

"I'm not lying!"

"I know you're not," said Steve perfunctorily, searching for the right questions. "What did you hear—anything?" Assume she saw something, maybe not what she described, but something that she could mistake it for in the dark. Well, with a long stretch of the imagination there are rocket backpacks now. They weren't good for much distance, but they could get to a waiting car. Maybe they had the backpacks on, they weigh a lot, that would explain the loping run, and maybe they had some kind of tarp with them that fluttered, and that could be wings—

A long, long stretch of the imagination. But Christ, if they were going to go to all that kind of trouble to dig up a corpse, they may have done something crazy like that.

"I'm sorry—" He'd missed her answer.

"It was a flapping sound."

"Like wings?"

"Like canvas fluttering."

"Any other sound?"

"No."

They drove back to the office in silence, but before Steve left he asked Mrs. Neal if she'd had her headlights on when she was driving out to get her dog. She said that she had.

"Is that important?" she asked.

Steve opened his car door. "It tells me that they knew you were coming even before the dog got there. And still they kept doing what they were doing—so they were determined to finish up whatever they were doing. They ran, after you got there, not before, or you never would have seen them."

In the light from the car's interior Steve could see the worry in the woman's eyes. He pulled out the medallion and held it up to her face. "Have you ever seen anything like this before?" he asked.

She shook her head.

"Never," said her husband. "Are you trying to imply something?"

"Not at all," said Steve; he could see the honesty in their eyes. He slipped the medallion back in his pocket and handed them both a business card. "But what this talisman tells me is that someone has come back for a visit of some kind. And what I would like you to do is try to keep an eye out, get a name, a license plate number, or something, if someone visits and you happen to see them. If you'll do that for me, I'll try to find out what you saw that night, Mrs. Neal, and hopefully catch the people who did this. Is it a deal?"

"A deal," she said. "I saw what I saw."

"I believe you saw what you saw, Mrs. Neal; but what I've got to do is find out what you saw. Goodnight," he said, and got into his car, started it, and waited for the caretaker to lead him down to the gate, and let him out, so he could head for home.

Seven

KAY AUDETTE

Steve arrived at his office at seven in the morning, pulling into his marked parking space under the building. Getting out of the car he noted that the near-empty garage contained a red Fiat Spider sports car. That would be Kay Audette's car, thought Steve. She was one of the new investigators he'd hired. She'd been with Brogan and Associates going on eleven months now. She was working out okay, he had heard.

Steve took the elevator up to the top floor and stepped out into a reception area. It was too early for Shirley to be in. Her unmanned reception desk faced him as he stepped out into the reception area. Brogan and Associates occupied the entire top floor. On the wall behind Shirley's desk was the company logo, a four-leaf clover with a medieval knight helmet in the center. Spelled out in block letters around the logo was:

Brogan and Associates, Security Services, Inc. To each side of the desk was a locked door.

Steve took his passkey from his pocket and let himself in, and walked down the corridor, turning on the fluorescent lights as he went.

He stopped in the staff room and looked back at the last desk. Kay Audette sat, smoking a cigarette, staring into her coffee. A half-eaten glazed donut sat on a white napkin near the phone. Brogan looked at her eyes and recognized a night person coping with early morning hours. She was dressed in a white silken blouse and black slacks.

"Good morning," Steve said.

"Oh, hi," Kay said. She seemed to perk up a bit. She indicated the phone with a scowl. "Skip-tracing. Back East. The damn time difference. I've been here since five." She sighed, shaking her head. "Steve, can't you get me something more interesting?"

"Ken handles assignments, Kay. You know that." He watched her wince, so he said, "He's said good things about your work."

"Well, y'know. As long as I'm last desk in this place, I get hand-me-down assignments, and the crap jobs. I want something exciting—or, okay, at least something that requires more than basic skills." She stopped, and eyed him, taking the measure of her words on him, then said, "You must have been last desk once. If you find something good, give me a chance, will you?"

Steve knew Kay's type. She was young, and

eager for some excitement. Steve had been that way, once, too. But his main concern was losing her to someone else's firm. She was good, and his company had put a lot of time and money into training her. He pulled his notebook from his back pocket. "When I started this business, I was the *only* desk," he said. "See what you can do with this." He read her the information on John Chadwick, including the fact that he'd served aboard a carrier during Viet Nam, but left out the fact that he had already located him, and that he had talked to his sister. "I need to know where this guy is. I need to know it without him knowing I know it. Okay?"

She grinned. "Yeah, sure. Thanks."

Don't thank me, thought Steve. Not yet. He wasn't sure if he was going to use her on this case. He needed someone with good instincts working with him, and he had never worked with Kay before to know if she had them. He was starting to have a crawling feeling about it, and the last time he had that feeling was at the beginning of the Balatta Sting case, and by the time it was concluded three of his best people had died.

"You've got a case?" Ken Anderson said, walking through Steve's open door.

Steve looked up over case review reports, and grinned. "Well, don't look so goddamn surprised. You're the one that gave away my hiding place to Veronica Dest—what the hell did you think she wanted from me, a kiss?"

Ken sat down in a plush chair near Steve's desk, sipping his morning coffee. He always reminded Steve of a puma, with his lithe catlike movement. He was a handsome black man in his middle thirties, former L.A.P.D., too. He'd quit the force to join Steve's company about seven years ago, and had been a real asset. After the Balatta Sting, Steve turned all the active case assignments over to Ken, and took care of administration. Ken was more than his right-hand man, he was a confidant and friend.

"It's about time," Ken said. "Telling you, man, me *carrying* you, doing *all* the work, is getting *old!*"

"Maybe I ought to give you my job then," Steve offered, knowing that Ken's idea of dying and going to hell, was to wake up behind a desk with a sign saying *Administrator* on his office door.

"Shee-*it!* You do, and I quit!"

Steve briefed Ken on the Chalmers case, then asked him if he could afford to lose Kay for a while to give him a hand.

"She's doing last-desk stuff. She's good enough. She's earned something better."

"How's her instincts?"

Ken stopped his cup inches from his lips, then lowered it without taking a sip. His face lost all expression. "I thought you said this was a simple case."

"It is, but I'm starting to get the crawl on this one. Itch I can't scratch. It might turn to shit. I don't know yet."

Ken considered this for a moment. "Well, she's getting antsy for some Mike Hammer action. I haven't had the heart to tell her that that's not very likely in this business. And I'm afraid if we don't let her have something, she'll start looking around."

"Yeah, that's what I was thinking, too . . ."

Kay Audette stomped into the room and threw a piece of paper on Steve's desk. She was livid. She stared at him, then at Ken, then back at Steve. "I don't need your charity!" She stuck a finger at the paper on his desk. "There's his address, phone number, and place of employment! Of course, you knew that all along, didn't you!"

"You better calm down," said Ken, his eyes wide in amazement. "That's the owner you're talking to."

She turned on Ken. "I don't have to take this! I asked for a little interesting work, and he gives me something he's already tracked. Some kind of kid's test!"

"What are you talking about?" Steve asked innocently. Part of being good at his job, was being a good actor. And for a moment she almost bought it, then her eyes flared. She pointed a finger at him. "You're Angel! The minute she said a man named Angel called about a reunion, I knew it was you!"

Steve raised his hands and waved toward a chair. "Sit down. And calm down too."

Her green eyes flicked, undecided, then she sat and crossed her arms across her chest, staring at him. Her eyes were filmed over. She's a proud person, Steve thought. He felt kind of bad that she was this upset. Still, he decided to press her. "I'm sorry," he said. "But I don't know what you're talking about."

Her resolve started to waver. An uncertainty in her eyes. "You do, too," she managed to say, then her eyes went hard. "You do, too. I really looked up to you. How could you even think of testing me about something so basic? You thought I couldn't con an address out of a talky sister?" She exhaled violently, then stared out the window. "I suppose I'm fired now, right? For standing up for myself."

Steve stood up. "On the contrary. I'm glad you are working with me on this case."

"Well, why waste my time with something you already know?" She was calming down now, Steve noted. Thank God. What a fireball.

"I knew that you could find out his address and phone number—"

She flipped her chin at him. "See, you *are* Angel. I knew it." A reflective look crossed her face for a moment, then she said, "Well, then, why'd you do it?"

Ken Anderson spoke in his low rumbling voice. "He was testing your instincts, Kay. So

75

don't beef. You passed the test." He looked at Steve.

Steve felt a big smile cut across his own face. "That's right, Ken," and then he said to Kay, "You still want on the case, or would you rather go skip-trace some deadbeats?"

"Work with you, of course," she said, then looked at Ken then back to him. *"Angel?"* She started to laugh. *"Angel?* Where in the hell did that name come from, a Dick Tracy comic book?" She took a cigarette from Ken, lit up, and broke into laughter again.

Relieved that Kay could laugh off what he'd done to her, Steve began to brief her on the Chalmers case.

Eight

GLASS HOUSE

After briefing Kay Audette on the Chalmers case, Steve sent her back to continue her normal routine until he found some part of the case for her to work on.

Ken Anderson hung around, getting up from the chair, turning his back on Steve, staring out the window. Steve watched his friend put his hands in his pockets and jangle his keys, a nervous habit that Steve had come to know meant Ken's thoughts were on serious matters. Steve reached into his own pocket and pulled out the amulet, and turned it over and over in his hands. He still hated the feel of it, perhaps caused by his general dislike of the occult, he thought. He put the charm down, and drew out a piece of stationery from his desk drawer, and began drawing the design pictured on both sides of the coin in a larger fashion on the paper.

"I never liked working cult cases," Ken said.

Steve looked up at him and saw that Ken had turned, his ebony profile lit by the morning sunlight. Steve watched Ken's brown eyes in erratic motion as they followed the traffic outside. The keys jangled. Steve waited patiently. Ken turned and faced him. "Steve, let me ask you, do you really have the crawl on this one? Because if you do, then let's just bail out. We lost too many good people last time. Let old Veronica Dest call in somebody else's favor."

Steve stared at Ken, hoping that the surprise and disbelief he was feeling wasn't showing. It was totally unlike Ken to want to duck out of an investigation.

"I understand how you feel, Ken, but I've committed to the preliminary investigation, anyway. Besides, The Grand Dame Chalmers has an interesting daughter. I've got to follow up on her, at least."

Ken grunted. "I was thinking about George and Bob and Jesse, that's all." He looked around Steve's office at empty brown chairs and a vacant crème-colored sofa. "I can still feel them here sometimes. Just talking. Shooting the shit the last time you got the crawl. I want 'em back sometimes. They were good people . . ."

His voice trailed off, and he sank down into a chair, and stared blankly at Steve's desk top.

Steve felt his heart hitch a little. For courage, and bravery, there was no finer man alive than Ken Anderson. And it wasn't like him to show this much feeling. He was normally a private man, but what he was telling Steve in a round-about way was that he didn't want anything to happen to Steve. Steve felt touched, and said to Ken, "If it turns to shit, pardner, we'll call in the cops, and we'll just sit back and let them take the heat."

Ken pondered this for a moment, then clapped his hands together as if to seal the deal. He stood up, and said as he walked toward the door, "Good. Because Mary said she'd tan your white ass if you got me mixed up in another shooting, and then she'd leave *me*."

Ken left, and Steve picked up the telephone and called L.A.P.D. Devonshire Division, and asked to talk to the investigating officer of the Chalmers case. Somehow it didn't surprise him when he was told that the case had been transferred downtown to the Parker Center, nick-named the Glass House because of the windows that made up its outside walls. It figured, with Mrs. Chalmers having that much pull, that it would be taken downtown to Robbery/Homicide, but what Steve hadn't expected was that Major Crimes had taken over the case. They were saved for celebrity murders, or serial killers. She must have some pull, this Chalmers.

He made another call, this one downtown, but not to Major Crimes. He didn't know anyone working that detail. Instead, he called his old buddy, Captain Ray Kent, who headed up the gang task force, and had him set Steve up with a Captain Roy B. Cowin, the prime mover in

Major Crimes. The appointment was for two-thirty.

Steve closed the Manila folder, and sat back in the chair.

"See," said Kathy Fandino, the detective who was handling the Chalmers investigation, "odds are a million to one against this leading to anything."

"I think you're right," Steve acknowledged, thinking to himself that her assessment was on the money. The reports and follow-ups really left nothing to go on. As usual, L.A.P.D. had done its job, and a good one at that. Steve half expected that the peculiar design shown on the medallion would show up somewhere in the photographs or investigation, thus establishing a link, but nothing of the kind appeared in the reports.

"This stuff is sick," said Fandino, reaching past Steve so that she leaned against him, and slowly stacking the four files on top of one another. "Especially the raping of the corpse. I don't see how any guy could get his rocks off by humping a woman dead some five years. Stupid, too. Now we've got the blood type off the semen. But that won't matter, unless something else pops. You be sure to let me know if you come across anything."

Steve smelled her sweet perfume, and was conscious of the light press of her body against his, as she now dug through her purse and pulled out a card. "Keep me informed," she said again, and handed him the card.

"You got it," said Steve, feeling guilty because he already was hiding something—the coin in his pocket. And what bothered him was that Kathy had been square with him. Most cops guard their cases with a personal vengeance—it's their work, after all. And Steve knew that even with a direct order from up above, some cops wouldn't have been as helpful as Kathy had. But, on the other hand there didn't seem to be a link after all. And if there was he could always phone her and let her know.

"Mrs. Chalmers wants to be sure that she's done everything possible. I told her L.A.P.D. would have done the job, but I think hiring me was for her conscience, or something like that. She can say to herself she's done everything that she could. Thanks for helping me out." Steve closed the small notebook in which he had jotted down a few notes and put it inside his coat pocket.

Then he made a decision. He reached into his pocket and pulled out the piece of paper with the pentagram design he copied off the medallion. "Have you ever seen anything like this?"

"Is it related?"

"Sort of. I'm working a cult angle. This is the kind of shit they might do."

"Doesn't ring any bells."

A meaty hand reached in and snatched the

paper. Steve turned and saw a short, fat detective in his fifties, wearing jeans and T-shirt. "I saw this about a week ago," he said.

"That's some rude shit," said Kathy. "Grabbing it like that."

"You want what I know, or don't ya?"

"Sure do," said Steve.

"Doing chicken-hawk check down at the bus station," he said. "Popped a guy, hadda tattoo like that on his chest."

"Exactly like it?" asked Steve.

The detective eyed him coldly. "I said that didn't I. I did a field interview report on him and kicked him loose."

"Can I see it?" asked Steve.

"Yeah. Why not."

The cop waddled away, and stopped at a desk piled high with cases and scattered paper, and started rooting through the mess.

"That Woodruff," said Kathy. "Good cop, but a pain in the ass."

Woodruff waddled back, and handed a piece of scratch paper, and said, "Two-time loser, but been no real trouble in ten years. Here's his address and phone number. I ran it and it's valid."

"Thank you very much," said Steve.

"No problem," said Woodruff and he waddled off fast as he had come.

Steve looked at the address. "Where is Hennington?"

Kathy said, "I don't know. You can look it up on a map."

"Yeah. When I get home." He slipped the paper into his coat pocket.

"Do you have a card?" asked Kathy. "We'll keep in touch."

Steve pulled out a card and handed it to her. "You looking for a job?" he joked.

"No. I'm looking for a date."

She had a half smile on her face that Steve couldn't read for sure. He didn't think she was kidding. The image of Molly's face briefly crossed his mind, a woman who had a boyfriend, and wasn't particularly fond of him. Still, why did she stick in his mind like that?

"Well, you've got my number," he said, rising, leaving it non-committal enough. The detective was his type: attractive, intelligent, and athletic. Maybe things with Molly wouldn't work out, and it'd be nice to have someone else to fall back on.

"Okay, I'll give you a call some time."

"Fine. And I'll keep you informed."

She smiled warmly and walked close to him as she escorted him out.

Nine

PIZZA

This is stupid, thought Steve, pulling out of the police parking structure and entering the beginning of the evening traffic rush. *Why should I feel guilty about being asked on a date? Molly has a boyfriend, has shown no interest in me, and Kathy's a dynamite woman that I would go out with in a second any other time. Damn!*

Still, he did feel guilty, and maybe that was why he wasn't going to call the Chalmers to make a report, but drop by on his way home—going *out* of his way on his way home, just to see Molly was the real story, he admitted to himself. God, how long had it been since he'd felt like this . . . since . . . since Constance.

Yes.

He tried to put that out of his mind and jacked up the radio. Jazz music filled the car, and he tried to lose himself in the notes, as he guided his car onto the freeway ramp, and down into the rush-hour crunch. He wouldn't get to the Chalmers place much before six o'clock at this rate.

Steve jockeyed the car into the fast lane, then crawled along with the other homeward-bound commuters, as he steered with one hand and made phone calls with his other.

He pulled his notebook from his coat with his right hand while steering with his left, and flipped through it, until he came to the number of Dr. Baruch Katzmer, the occult specialist who had been recommended by the police department. He dialed and managed to squeeze in under the closing-time deadline at the County Museum. Dr. Katzmer was not in, but his secretary was and Steve made an appointment for the next day at one-thirty in the afternoon.

Next, Steve called his office, getting Ken Anderson and Kay Audette on a conference line. He gave Kay the name and address of Floyd Carlson, in Hennington, California, told her about the tattoo on his chest, and asked her to investigate him and see if the tattoo had any significance to Carlson other than for body design. He smiled at her bubbly reply, "Get right on it, Steve."

"One thing more, Kay," said Steve.

"What?"

"Ken is your control. Check in with him at least once a day, even if it's nothing new. And be careful, okay?"

There was a moment of silence. "I'll be real careful," she said.

"Good," said Steve. "Careful people live longer." And as he said it, he thought of Bob, George, and Jesse, and how they had been careful people, and how they had died.

Molly stood in the parlor and held the phone to her ear long after her ex had hung up on her. The thought, *the bastard, the bastard,* kept pacing through her mind. He was selfish then, and he is selfish now, she thought as she re-cradled the phone. How could anyone turn down the need of a child? He could. He did. The bastard! And though he didn't say it his tone conveyed the message: she's not my child and you're a slut.

Molly blinked back tears. What was she going to do? Duffy's last fit had been the worst yet. Molly thought that if Duffy had one that was any more severe, she would have to put her in the hospital.

The girls giggling brought her back to reality. She heard the deep rumbling of Steve Brogan's voice, followed by another gale of laughter from the girls. She wished they would laugh like that with Thom. Maybe, in time.

She straightened her shoulders and checked her face in the mirror. She passed. Thank God for waterproof mascara.

Molly found Steve Brogan in the parlor where

she had left him. He had called before coming over, evidently counting on catching Carlotta in when he delivered the information on John to Molly, so that she would be updated as well. But Carlotta was at her Republican women's meeting and wouldn't be home before nine. Molly had explained this to him, but he said he would hang around to see if Molly needed any follow-up work done after the phone call. At least that's what he had said, though she suspected a different reason than that from him. When she entered the room and they made eye contact, she felt his interest in her, burning in his eyes.

"Well," he asked, leaving off anything else for the sake of the children.

She shook her head.

"Anything else you want me to do about it?"

She shook her head, finally regaining complete control. "No," she said. "It was like I told Carlotta it would be." Steve's look of disappointment at the news touched her. She continued, "I don't believe Carlotta will be back for some time," she said. "You can tell me, and I'll relay the information, but I'm sure she'll want to hear it from you, anyway."

Steve checked his watch. "Well, it's dinnertime. Would you and the girls," he squinted mischievously at her two daughters, "like to be my guests at Chuck-E-Cheese for some pizza and games?"

The girls exploded in a singsong chorus of,

"Yes, yes, please Mom, yes," (probably just as Steve Brogan had intended, Molly figured), and since he had been so helpful, how could she do anything but say, "Yes."

Steve poured himself some more beer from the pitcher, and took another bite out of a slice of pepperoni and mushroom pizza. Molly was using the restroom, and the girls were playing video games, running around in the swirl of kids that put this place in motion. It felt good to be with a family again, even if he had had to force it some—okay, a lot. And yes, he had been kind of sneaky, and a bit underhanded, using the girls to get Molly out socially—but he liked her, darn it; and the girls, too.

No court in the world would convict him of wrongdoing, anyway. The kids were having a great time, and after an initial quiet period Molly had perked up, and started talking about the girls, how well they were doing in school, her job, and general things, the way people do when they're getting to know each other.

Molly walked by and sat down across from him. "Did the girls report in?" she asked.

"Yes, once," he answered. "They'd won enough yellow tickets to buy out that gift kiosk." Steve pointed to the booth where the kids exchanged their tickets for toys.

Molly laughed, took a sip of beer, then canted

her head and asked, "Are you tired of answering questions about the sting thing you were in?"

"Not for you, I'm not." Steve found himself staring into his beer. "Not much they wrote about it was true; not much of the personal stuff, especially."

"It's okay. Just pass on it. I didn't want to get you upset."

"No, really. Ask me, I'll tell you anything, really."

Molly fiddled with the ring on her finger for a moment and finally spoke. "I find it hard to believe that a man who is as good as you are with the girls, would put . . ." she halted and looked embarrassed as she realized how what she was asking was going to sound.

Steve understood immediately what was going on; she was going to ask about Constance and her kids, and how could he have endangered their lives during the Balatta Sting. Oh, how the tabloids had done a job on him.

"Go on and ask," he said, hearing the deadly rattle in his tone himself. "About the kids, right?"

"I'm sorry." Molly blanched.

"No. I'm sorry. I told you to ask anything, forgetting that some things are just too ugly to ever go away. What you read in the papers was fabrication, because I wouldn't talk about it. So they made up lies. They said that my wife divorced me because I put her life and those of her children—they were from a previous mar-

89

riage—in danger during the Balatta Sting. That's what you read, right?"

"Yes." She was listening intensely, an odd look in her eye.

"Well, let me tell you what happened. Constance is a very bright woman, and not used to following orders. I was in the middle of the Sting and I needed a control. Do you know what a control is?" Molly shook her head "no." "Okay, a control is an element of an operation who is not directly involved, but who monitors it from afar. If anything goes awry, it is the control that will call the shots on the contingency backup . . ."

"Like calling in the Mounties to the rescue." Molly offered.

"Exactly," said Steve. "No involvement in the operation at all, yet, aware of all the activities, so that if certain people don't check in, etc., help can be called in.

"Constance wanted to be part of the business, and I put her off and off, until she was furious. When she heard about the control concept, she wanted that position. I made a mistake in giving in to her. I knew she was willful, but the control concept is so simple, yet so important, I just knew that she could follow the concept, and would follow the edicts of the position—it is that important.

"Well, to make a long story short, as control, she reviewed the operation in progress, and decided that I had handled it all wrong; so without consulting me, approached Balatta on her own, thus blowing cover on several of my agents, resulting in their murders, and directing Balatta's hit men at her, and of course, her children. She nearly cost me my life on top of that, that stubborn woman." Steve shook his head, feeling the intensity of heartache he had felt at that time once again.

"So you divorced her," Molly said, not unkindly.

"No. I could have forgiven her," he said. "But she could never forgive herself—she divorced me."

"And you covered for her with the newspapers."

"Exactly. She's a proud woman . . ."

"Who let you take the blame for a wrong that she's responsible for. I wouldn't sing her praises too loudly, Steve. Take it from me. You are better away from a woman who would let you take such a big fall for her. Duffy's father is the same kind of man—too proud to be a Christian to admit that he fathered a child; and Penny's father, the great Dr. Daniels, studying baboons in Africa, who can't take time to be responsible, to raise a family. People who are responsible are what hold families and governments, and everything else together." She slapped the table firmly, her eyes fiery, her lips pressed together, and then let loose with a tiny smile. "I guess I made a speech, didn't I?"

Steve grinned. "Yes, you did. And I loved it!"

They both laughed, and Steve told her that it was his turn. He asked about Thom. "He seems so somber," Steve said. "And you're so full of life. How long have you been seeing him?"

Molly's face sobered up immediately at the mention of Thom's name. She leaned forward as if making a point. "He's not a flighty person like my John or Tim—I've had it up to here with the here-today, gone-tomorrow types. He's dependable, and bright enough to be interesting."

"What does he do?"

"Real estate. Done well with it, too."

"You're going to get married?"

"He hasn't asked, but he wants me to meet his family, soon."

The girls had called him Thom-the-Bomb, Steve remembered, when he had asked them about him. They didn't like him at all. "How does he do with the girls? They get along okay?" Steve wondered if she would lie to him.

Molly cleared her throat before she spoke. "Actually, they don't relate as well as I would like. They'll come around I'm sure. He's a very stable man."

The kids ran up all excited, waving a fistful of yellow tickets. Steve and Molly escorted them to the gift kiosk, where they traded the tickets for candy suckers and soft toys.

Steve drove them home. Carlotta was still out, and Steve said his good-byes out on the porch. Duffy and Penny hugged him tightly and kissed him on the cheek. Molly shook hands with him, and said, "Thank you for a nice time. I'm glad we talked, and I'm glad that you're handling Carlotta's case."

"Well, thank you, too," Steve said, "for a nice evening out. Tell Carlotta I'll be in touch. Bye, girls."

The girls giggled, and a few minutes later, as he drove away, he thought that he should have told Molly that Thom wasn't the only stable man around. He should have said, "I'm stable. And the girls *like* me."

what horrible task Floyd actually was a ... ning
he asked for him and ... as your ... iection
Carlson says ... ection ... he past
will me ... you me ... away and ... or a ...
... ing ... you ... ver ... Th ... e Th ...

Ten

THE CAVERNS

Near noon, Dwight Kleiber pulled into Floyd Carlson's Chevron station and parked right in front of the office. He got out and walked into the garage to a closed back door and banged on it twice.

"Who in the fuck is it?" came Floyd's reedy voice.

"Sorry to disturb you, Floyd," said Dwight, not sorry at all. He heard scrambling, and the door popped open, and Floyd Carlson stood before him. He was a small man with a head that appeared even smaller still for the size of his body. His oily dark hair and shifty brown eyes were the same as the day Dwight had met him in the attorney's room in Los Angeles. It had been Lady Eva who had hired him to defend the little squirt, to get him off on a pandering charge, involving minors. It wasn't until he was totally dedicated to Eva that he learned exactly what horrible task Floyd actually was performing for her.

"Oh, sorry, Dwight. I didn't know it was you," Floyd said, and stepped aside. Dwight pushed passed him into the room and sat down at Floyd's desk.

"Coffee, Dwight?" offered Floyd, the obsequious tone tickling Dwight. Ever since the announcement of his installation at the right hand of Eva, everyone around had been even more respectful to him than they had been before.

"No, Floyd," said Dwight. "I am being installed tonight, remember?"

"Yes. That's right. Everybody's going to be there. And you can't drink or eat all day, that's right."

Dwight fished into his pocket and pulled out one of the medallions. He handed it to Floyd, who almost choked at the sight of it. "Does Lady Eva know you have this?" he asked.

"Who are you to question me, Floyd?" said Dwight in a slow, deadly cadence. He relished watching the blood drain out of the small man's face. "You are good at procuring girls for the brood, and that's about it. You nearly got caught the last time, right? You're lucky they only took down your name, and even that's too much to bear, right? I can find someone else to fill your spot, can't I? Who are you to question me?"

His fear made him stammer at first. "I—I—I was wrong to question you . . . I—I mean I wasn't questioning you. I was just shocked to see the sacred coin up close . . . I—"

"Pick it up, and put it in your pocket," ordered Dwight. Floyd did so. "I want you to take Gilbey and go to this place." He handed him a slip of paper. "Follow my instructions to the letter." Dwight gave him the instructions, just as Eva had given him the instructions. Floyd's eyes went wide as Dwight finished the orders. "The time of the Gathering is near. There is much to be done, and the rewards will be great for all of us. We will need new brood women soon, too. But first do as I say. Do it tomorrow night. Drive down to the city. Use one of the safe cars. If you get interrupted you can ditch the car, and fly home. Understand?"

"Yes, Dwight," said Floyd. "Just one thing, though. Can I take Cutter or Radd, instead of Gilbey. Gilbey's so damn dumb, if there's a hitch—"

"Cutter and Radd are with Sloat somewhere. Sloat won't even be at my installation. He's off taking care of some matters for Lady Eva. Besides Gilbey's strong; take him."

Dwight stood up, indicating the talk was over. Floyd trailed him out to his car. "See you tonight," he said, "and congratulations on the installation—you deserve it."

Dwight got into his car. "Yes, I do," smiled Dwight. "Don't I?"

"You surely do, Dwight," fawned the mechanic. "I'll take care of that chore you gave me quick and clean, don't you worry."

Dwight nodded and drove away, turned right and head out of town up higher into the mountains towards the Caverns.

In the daylight, Dwight was escorted up near the mouth of the cavern by the guard jeep. He parked and made his way through a stand of young pine trees to the entrance. A huge robed man stepped out from near a granite boulder holding an M-16 assault rifle.

"Hello, Bork," said Dwight.

"Mr. Kleiber," said Bork, the deference in his voice exhilarating Dwight.

Bork followed Dwight as he wove around several boulders toward the entrance of the cave. "Bork, as Keeper of the Cave, I expect you at the installation," said Dwight, knowing full well that Bork would automatically be required to attend the ceremony. He said it to let Bork know that he valued him.

Bork's response satisfied him greatly. "It is an honor to be in your presence, Mr. Kleiber," the big man said. "It is also an honor to be witness to your installation."

They arrived in a cleared spot before an opening in the granite face of a forty-foot cliff. It was the size of a two-car garage door, the largest of three openings in a fifty-foot stretch. The one to the right a man could walk through stooping, and one to the left was very small—a child could crawl through. All led into a large natural antechamber that acted as a security/reception area.

Two of Bork's armed men stood from behind the reception desk as they entered, and sat back down as Dwight made his way past the desk to tunnels leading down into the bowels of the caverns. Bork accompanied Dwight down the tunnel. "It still amazes me," said Dwight as his eyes adapted to the dim yellow light provided by frosted-glass enclosed light bulbs. "It is as if this whole cavern had been designed specifically for the Coven."

"Yes," Bork's voice rumbled. "Designed by the Dark One, M'Lady Eva once told me. The Great Jobina first saw it, and directed the Coven here."

"Impressive," Dwight said, reminded by Bork's mention of Jobina, Lady Eva's predecessor, that Bork had been with the Coven since the Beginning.

They walked for a few minutes through a passageway that entered into the great cathedral where the meetings were held. The main cavern was big enough to easily handle a thousand people. It had a natural slant to it, and the Coven had modified it slightly, making it a series of terraced slopes down. Large stalactites hung everywhere, and down at the lowest point, where the cavern formed the natural stage, nature had provided an outpouring of white and rose quartz, that was called the Veil of Tears, that provided a stone curtain around the stage.

It was lit by incandescent bulbs, but during a ceremony candles were lit, and the effects were stunning.

A group of five young women down by the staging area practiced for the installation. They wore pink silk robes and moved in a circle around a pentagram inlay of white marble in the center of the stage. They began to chant, a rhythmic alto incantation, unaware of Dwight's and Bork's presence.

Bork flashed his light up into the top of the caves, excusing himself as he did so. "Want to check . . . yeah, the pipes. See those red pipes . . ."

Dwight saw more than that. Venting ducts and electrical conduits and several different colored pipes were hidden up there. Without the light one could see nothing. He spotted the red one, easily. "What about it?" Dwight asked.

"It's a gas pipe. I hated to send it down the middle like I did, but had to do it. I have howler boxes up there every ten feet that will detect a leak. Eva needs the gas for the ovens. In the end it was the safest way."

Dwight sensed a need of approval from Bork so he said, "I'm sure you have done the best for the needs of Lady Eva and the Coven, Bork. I trust your judgment."

A smile cut its way across Bork's face. "Thank you, Mr. Kleiber," he said and cut off the light. "That means a lot coming from you."

Once again, Dwight felt that rush of exuberance that he felt when shown deference by those who recognized his position.

They proceeded down the smooth gentle slope of the cavern toward the part that would be considered the stage area—the place where Dwight would be installed as Eva's right-hand man.

As they reached the stage, thirteen giggling young women, dressed in hooded lime green robes made of an ephemeral material, skittered from one of the rear openings, and made their way to center stage. They took up positions in a circle surrounding the large white marble pentagram embedded in the floor of the stage. In their hands they held black candles. One girl moved to the inner part of the circle, lit her candle from the gas-fed eternal flame in the center of the pentagram, then stepped back. One by one the others did the same, then, when all candles were lit they began to chant and sway rhythmically in a side-to-side motion back and forth.

"These are your maidens," Bork said. "They are practicing for the ceremony tonight. Lady Eva chose them herself. Are they not lovely?"

Dwight smiled. "I'm not sure. They still have their robes on."

Bork laughed and said, "Trust me, Lord Kleiber, I have seen them practice the entire ceremony. You will be pleased."

"I am pleased with anything Lady Eva has

prepared for me, Bork." Dwight faced the stage fully, and commanded, "Skyclad. Skyclad."

The women did not miss a beat, swaying and releasing their robes and tossing them behind them, and almost in unison the gowns fluttered to the cavern floor. The women began skipping around the pentagram in a circle, and as each approached the point closest to Dwight, she turned, and opened her arms toward him, then turned back to the flow of the circle's motion.

"She did choose well, Bork," Dwight said, and he meant it. Lady Eva had chosen a mixture of ages and body shapes and races. He liked variety, and tonight each of them would be sworn in blood loyalty to him. They would die to please him, and kill to save him.

Dwight turned to Bork. "And the bucks?" he said, referring to the male counterparts to the maidens.

"Thirteen men, strong and willing to do your bidding, Lord Kleiber. They will be rehearsing the ceremony in about an hour if you want a preview."

"Thank you, Bork. You may go about your duties."

Bork bowed and headed back up toward the entrance.

Dwight took a last glance at the maidens, and turned and walked toward a tunnel opening to the side of the stage. He was pleased. Twenty-six men and women to live and die at his command. By the end of the installation, the thought of disobeying him would be anathema to their minds. The only person able to thwart his instruction to them would be Lady Eva herself—and perhaps Sloat.

As he headed through the dimly lit tunnel he wondered if Sloat would be a problem to him. Dwight decided that Lady Eva would have that end of it under control before she installed Dwight, and that it did him no good to dwell on it. He had other things to think about, like Anna, and the Sacrifice.

Still, as he reached the bifurcation, the left of which led to the hatcheries, the thought of Sloat clung to him like something wet and cold.

He took the hatcheries tunnel, and began to whistle softly as he headed toward the amp ward. That's the ward that held Anna. Sweet, sweet, misguided Anna.

All of this could have been yours, he thought, as wife to the High Priest of the Coven you would have been denied nothing—except our first-born child, and that we are going to lose anyway.

As he passed the first hatchery ward, he heard the grunt and screams of lovemaking, mingled with the cries of the newborns. When he reached the second opening, the amp ward hatchery, he walked in and found the chamber deserted. *They're getting sunned,* he thought. It was for their health. Once a day they were escorted to a sunning pen on the far side of the cavern. He was turning to go when he heard the sudden cries of his infant son, and Anna's admonitions for him to stop.

He stood for a moment listening to them. His ex-wife Anna, who had not wanted to give up her infant to the Glory of Coven, and his son, Dwight's ticket to everlasting power, squealing and blubbering the way babies do. He strode to the far end of the chamber where the screwing cribs were. Most were semi-private, but one had a curtain across it. *Even in her shame they treat her special,* he thought, *Because of me. They're afraid I'll find some sympathy, and punish them for mistreating her. I'll put a stop to this, when the Tender gets back from sunning the amps.*

Dwight started to enter when he heard Anna speak to the baby in a voice emotional with tears. "I'll not let them use you like that. I'll strangle you myself, rather than see you butchered like that . . ."

Without the child, Dwight could not be installed. It would mean impregnating another woman, and waiting for term. NO! Dwight pushed the rough curtain aside and rushed into the chamber.

It was cramped and Dwight had to stand over Anna's bed, bent at the shoulders. He reached down quickly and snatched his baby son from her dangerous hands. She screeched, "NO-O-O!" in protest, reaching after the child. He kicked her in the face knocking her back in the bed. Blood dripped down from her newly split lip.

"Behave, or I'll have Dr. Sturgeon make another Fanny Funbag out of you!" Dwight growled. "Do you understand me?!" The threat was real and he could tell Anna knew it. When Fanny Talbert had tried to escape twice, Anna had ordered her legs and arms amputated at the trunk. And for her to be cared for and used as a sexual toy. She had become quite the vogue, and the men of the Coven (and some of the women) openly bragged about abusing her. For a time she became quite the fashion at orgies, too, the most outrageous of which Dwight had heard about was that after the group had finished with her, they had left her hanging from the ceiling in a love basket, smeared her with chicken guts and let the participant's dogs lick and jump, working themselves into a frenzy as Fanny swung and twisted all around screaming her head off as the dogs barked up a storm.

"Fanny Funbag?" he repeated, this time smiling.

He watched the fear twist Anna's still-lovely face into a contorted mask. Her full head of black hair fell about her in a shimmering corona accenting her pale face and blue, blue eyes. She was wearing a pink cotton gown, that covered her to just below the groin. Her right leg had been cut off at the torso and her left at the knee for trying to escape the Coven.

Dwight began rocking the child in his arms to quiet him. "You had it all, Anna," he said. "You were a respected member of the ruling elite of this Dark Miracle, groomed to reach the same heights as I am, and you blew it because you were selfish." He held the baby out from him as if to show her something. "This is not a terrible thing for him; there is no greater glory than to serve as Sacrifice to the Coven. Witches will sing his praises for eternity—he will rise again in another life as a prince. And you would take this honor from him? Or was it from me you wanted to steal?"

Anna turned her face away from him and mumbled something.

"What?" Dwight asked. He grabbed her breast and squeezed it hard until she screamed. "Look at me!"

She turned back to him. "I said, I hope you burn in hell."

"Like you won't, Miss Goody Two Shoes? You've sinned enough in this lifetime for an entire nation."

"But not anymore. I've asked God for forgiveness, and He's forgiven me."

Dwight stared at her in horror and clutched his son to his chest. "You blaspheme after all I've done for you? You ingrate." He backed out of the crib, halting just for a moment before he was free of her vileness. "Fanny Funbag, it is, Anna. You deserve it, you ungrateful bitch."

He turned and left her crib, to Anna's screams. "Don't kill our son! Don't kill our son, Dwight! In God's name, don't do it!"

Women! thought Dwight as he left the amp ward, and sought out his maidens, to care for the child. He made a mental note to call Doc Sturgeon and have him schedule Anna's surgery for tomorrow.

Eleven

—ESCAPE—

"You bastard!" Anna screamed at Dwight, but only after he had left the room, because the Fanny Funbag threat had taken its toll on her. She knew that he had meant what he said. Tomorrow it would be surgery for her, and she'd be just like Fanny Funbag after she'd healed up, used and abused even more than she was being used now.

"Goddamn you, Dwight!" she screamed again, convulsing in her bed. "I'll get you, fucker!"

She dropped limp in her bed, and thought about her baby. How could Dwight do such a thing, after all they'd been through to conceive the child.

She lay back in her bed and regained her composure. There would be time for tears later. Right now, she had to go over what she had been planning for a month, now—her escape. She had planned to take the baby with her, but now, she knew she could not recover her son. The best she could do was save herself, if she were lucky. And she would be doing it while Dwight was being installed. Everyone's attention would be fixed on the ceremony. Everyone would be in attendance, except for a skeletal staff, primary in the external security arena. But she had planned around them. Having been a High Priestess in the Coven, she knew much that the lowly guards did not, and she would use that to help her elude them.

Anna heard the clamor of the others returning from being sunned. She had gotten out of it herself, by telling Langdon, the Tender, that the baby wasn't up to it, and that he had best remain inside so that he would be up to tonight's ceremony. He hadn't questioned her at all about this, nor the other times she had begged off the sunning. She had used that time to devise some simple tools that she would use in her escape attempt.

"Pull it aside," Anna heard Fanny Funbag say.

"Okay."

Handsome Jake's voice.

The curtain to her crib parted in a scattering sound of curtain rings. Handsome Jake blocked most of the lower half of the entrance. He was a goodlooking, smart man. Too smart for his own good—he'd gotten caught sexing up Bruce Taylor's thirteen-year-old daughter without benefit of Coven Ritual, and since he was handsome and bright, Lady Eva had ordered his legs removed and for him to serve as stud for those women in the coven who wanted children without the hassle of being married.

Bruce Taylor, who had not been satisfied with the punishment meted out to Handsome Jake, regularly came down to the breeding cribs, turned Handsome Jake on his stomach, put him in restraints, and sodomized him. He told anyone who would listen, how he had renamed Handsome Jake, Homophobic Jake, and that his screams were music to his ears.

A double-leg amputee, H.J., as he was called for short, got around on a square piece of board, affixed with four skate wheels beneath and two hand blocks with which he reached down and scooted himself along. Langdon had fixed up a makeshift red wagon that he pulled along. In the wagon, set in a wooden brace, Fanny Funbag reigned queen over him by giving him orders. "Move the damn thing closer," she ordered.

H.J. twisted around and pulled the wagon up next to him. Fanny Funbag stared at Anna with bright green eyes. Her hair was a scraggly blond mess on the top of her head. She was dressed in a dingy red torso sack that was tied loosely at the throat. Her torso was perpendicular to Anna, so Fanny Funbag had to turn her head in an uncomfortable twist that strained her facial expression. She grinned a toothless, gummy black maw at Anna, giggled, then said, "I heard Dwight say you and me gonna be twins, Anna. Personally, I was hoping for a male, like poor old Freddy before his accident with the Rott-weiler."

Anna's mouth felt dry. She shifted her gaze to H.J., and the look in his eyes. She'd seen it before, when he had attacked Susie in the open ward, and raped her to the cackling glee of most of the other amputees.

"Yeah," Fanny Funbag was saying. *"You* are gonna be *sore,* the first year or so, Anna. And I don't mean your *stumps."* She broke into loud laughter, and it was then that H.J. reached in and stroked Anna's half leg with his oily hands.

"Don't!" Anna said, knowing the score already. The baby was gone, Dwight was obviously pissed at her. Now, no one was afraid that he might be angry if anyone messed with her, his ex. He had ordered her funbagged, so she was open game. And Anna had no illusions: in this place, there were those who did it, and those who had it done to them; predators and prey—strictly survival of the fittest. And right now, H.J. was sure he was gonna be the first to stick it to her.

Anna reached to the side of the bed and worked her fingers down between the mattress and the wooden box frame, and found the sawed-off broom pole with a roughly sharpened tip that she had talked Langdon into giving her to scratch her stump (but that in fact was part of her escape plans).

H.J. let go and smiled then stood up on his stumps and dropped his pants, exposing a huge fleshy erection. He arched back readying his attack and . . .

Anna lashed out, sitting up and extending the pole in a continuous motion, jabbing him with deadly accuracy right in the scrotum, tearing the sack and compressing his right testicle past the point of tolerable pain.

He screamed and clutched his groin, and Anna jabbed him in the right eye with the stick, and he jerked back in a twisting motion that tumbled him out of his skateboard, knocking Fanny Funbag violently out of her cradle as he fell. She tumbled over the side of the wagon, hit the floor and slid head-first screeching into the stone wall.

Anna quickly tucked the stick back in its hiding place and scrambled to the foot of her bed and pointed at the moaning H.J.

"And don't forget that, you scumbag."

The others, mostly women, mostly pregnant with altar babies, limped, hobbled, rolled, or crawled towards her end of the ward. Within seconds, Langdon ran into the room, and rushed through, the amputees scattering to the floor like dolls as he went.

He stopped in front of the two injured people and put his hands on his wide hips. He alternated, looking between Homophobic Jake and Fanny Funbag, all the while making *tsk-tsk-tsk* sounds. Finally, he glanced at Anna. "What happened?" he asked.

Anna was ready for him. She smiled sweetly and motioned him closer, closer.

Langdon waddled over pulling up on his pants belt, his ring of keys jiggling noisily.

"Come in," Anna said, and made a face like she was in pain. She backed up and sat against the headboard.

Langdon entered, his mass filling the whole entrance.

"Pull the curtain," she told him.

He was crammed in, and stooped over. "No. Tell me what."

Anna motioned him forward.

Langdon leaned in. "What happened, Anna?"

Anna bent forward at the waist. She knew Langdon was like H.J., and it was only a matter of time before he came for her, too. Probably want to rape her before the surgery. But he wouldn't do it now, he was too busy.

Anna said in a soft voice. "You know what's going to happen to me tomorrow, don't you?"

"Yeah," he said and smiled.

"Well, H.J. wanted to fuck me, and I didn't want him to. I've only got one night the way I am, and I wanted to spend it with you. Anything you want, and I do it willingly. You've been decent to me since I've been here, Langdon, and I want it to be you who gets the reward."

Langdon jolted in surprise, banging his bald head on the roof of the crib. "Ow," he said, ducked lower and rubbed it with a fat palm, all the time looking at Anna. "Okay," he said finally. "That'd be nice. But I got a lot of work to do for the installation. I'm chanting verses for it. But fucking you would be nice. I never like making women do it."

"What time do you go to the installation?"

"Nine. Why?"

"You come to me at eight-thirty, and I'll send you out a happy man, I promise. Your work'll be done by then. Then, you can come back afterwards if you're not too tired."

Langdon stared at her. He blinked dumbly at her, then nodded his head. "Eight-thirty, then," he said. "And thanks."

He left the crib, and Anna exhaled a heavy sigh. She watched Langdon pick up Fanny Funbag and carry her away, saying to H.J., "Shaddup your griping, you big baby. I'll be back for you."

After the dinner feeding, it was all that Anna could do to keep from crawling to the foot of the bed and looking out the crib bay into the ward every five minutes to make sure Langdon was still there. Her biggest fear was that he would leave, and get too wrapped up in something else, and then have to rush to Dwight's installation ceremony before he came to her.

Finally, after an intolerable amount of time, she reached under her pillow and pulled out a small ladies' wristwatch sans wrist. She had talked Langdon into getting it for her by telling him that she needed it to keep track of the baby's feeding times.

The hands of the watch read nearly eight-thirty. Normally at this time, there would be a lot of noise as members of the Coven would be traipsing in and out as they serviced the women of the breeding wards, or got serviced by the men; but tonight was the installation and there would be no grunting noises, laughter or screams.

The unusual silence put Anna's nerves on edge. What if Langdon left before he visited her? What if he did that? Then her plan was wrecked.

The lights went out, and Anna heard Langdon shout down the ward, "I'm warning you all; if there are any problems while I'm at the installation, you will know pain worse than childbirth."

Then an eerie silence ensued. He'd left.

Anna scrambled to the foot of the bed and stuck her head out of the curtain. In the dim butter-colored safety light she could see the empty ward. He was gone! Shit!

She rolled back and flopped on the bed. Now what was she going to do? Even if she got out of the cave, she needed . . .

The curtains parted and Langdon's huge mass, barely backlit by the dim safety lights in the ward, filled the doorway as a giant black silhouette. He closed the curtains behind him, and whispered, "We must be quick."

Relief flooded Anna. "Of course," she whispered back. "And I won't tell anyone, so you won't get in trouble."

When he had entered and whispered, she had understood instantly. Langdon still feared Dwight, and he did not want to risk his wrath, so he had left and come through the small, rear entrance, just outside and to the left of the crib. He whispered, to minimize the risk of someone in the ward knowing what he was about.

Anna said, "I was so worried. I thought that you forgot, or worse, didn't desire me." Was he buying it? she wondered.

"Oh, I wouldn't forget," he said, like a little boy confessing love for the first time to a girl. "I've . . . I've always . . . liked you, Anna."

A tender heart in this fat buffoon, thought Anna. Who would've guessed it?

"I thought so," said Anna. "I wanted to show you that I cared for you before tomorrow. Y'know?" She crawled to the end of the bed and took his large, callused hand, and guided him around to the side of the bed.

"Yeah," he said, his voice husky with lust. "Sorry about the amputations. Maybe he'll change his mind." He leaned forward and grabbed her head.

"Too rough," she said, jockeying into a sitting position on the edge of the bed. His big stomach was at her eye level and she reached up and grabbed his belt. "I want to do everything. I don't want you to have to work at all." She reached out, found his zipper, and unzipped his pants.

He moaned and she could feel his erection growing inside his pants. "I'm going to kiss it first," she said, "but don't come, because I want that inside. I want my next baby to be yours."

"Uh . . . okay. But don't tell Dwight. Just tell him it was dark and you didn't know who it was."

"I'll tell him H.J. did it, if he asks. He deserves it."

"Yeah. Perfect."

Langdon sounded relieved, and now Anna made her move. She reached inside his pants and through the fly opening of his boxer shorts and fondled his fat worm of a penis then pulled its hardening shaft out of the pants and put it in her mouth. He began thrusting with his hip, and she took the motion by backing up her head in time to his thrusts; otherwise she would gag. She moaned and shoved her head deep on him, at the same time running her hands back to his giant ring of jingling keys. They felt hard and rough as she ran her hands over them, and then further back on his belt where he kept his personal keys to his house and most importantly, his car, on a clip key ring. She moaned loudly to cover any noise and unclipped the personal keys, then dropped her hand quickly to her side and buried them under the mattress. She immediately put her hand on his penis and began upstroking to delay his ejaculation. She didn't want him coming in her mouth for one thing (it was repulsive enough to have to blow him), and the other was that she wanted to keep him here as long as possible so that he would have to rush out of her crib, too concerned with getting to the installation on time, so that he wouldn't notice that his smaller set of keys was missing. If he discovered it during the ceremony, he would know where he "dropped" them and figure that it was an accident and go back and get them after Dwight's installation. The thought that she would try to escape wouldn't occur to him because everyone knew it was an impossible task.

And she was going to do it!

She pulled her mouth off of him and unbuckled his belt and dropped his pants, then shucked down his boxer shorts. She told him to lie down on his back, and guided him back on the bed. His mass took up the whole bed, but it was easy enough to find his penis. "It's a good thing I had a baby, Langdon, or I don't think I'd be able to fit you inside me."

Langdon just moaned, and Anna slipped off her dress and mounted him, bending forward and lying across his stomach and chest, pushing with her half leg so that her torso moved up and down.

The friction with his penis was tremendous and she felt herself aroused in spite of herself. He clutched her to him and moaned as he came, and told her he loved her.

"I love you, too," she lied, and thought that

117

it was the least she could say, because if she got away with it, Evil Eva was going to have her deadly fun with him, that was for sure.

They lay for a moment in silence, and then suddenly, Langdon rose up knocking Anna to the side. "The Transformation!" He stood up suddenly and knocked his head on the low ceiling. "OW! AH! SHIT!"

He scrambled searching for his pants.

"Hold still!" Anna said in a harsh whisper. "I've got your pants. And be quiet. You just woke up half the ward."

She helped him dress and he went rushing out. He would still have to get to the robing area, and he rushed out of the crib with the fear of the Devil in him.

"I hope he fucked you dead," H.J. yelled down the ward.

"Yeah," Fanny Funbag sang out.

Others joined in, but in a while the noise in the ward died down, and Anna looked at the glow dials on her watch—five to nine. Old Langdon would just make it in time, she thought. Good for him. She reached down and pulled out his keys—and good for me.

At ten-thirty, Anna wrapped her stump in a rough fashion with a section of blanket, using a piece of torn cloth as belt and another piece tied around the material and then up to her belt to hold it in place. She was going to be walking on it for a long distance, and she wanted to protect the stump as much as possible.

She tore a hole in the center of the remaining piece of blanket and put her head through it to form a makeshift serape. It would be cold in the night air.

Finally she pulled out her sharpened broom pole, and from under her mattress an inch-thick piece of board three inches by five inches that she had worked loose from the bed frame. In its center she had fashioned a hole just a little smaller than the full diameter of the pole. She had worked three small nails loose from the frame also and used them to laboriously drill holes in the pole. She now assembled the device: an extension, meant to be held by hand, with which she could depress the gas pedal and brake on Langdon's Buick Skylark.

Everyone knew the car because Langdon had painted it a violet color with black polka dots the size of baseballs scattered all over it like the chickenpox. Langdon's explanation was that he thought it looked good. Everyone else thought it was because he was dimwitted.

To move she needed both hands and her partial leg, so she affixed a torn cloth strap to the hand pole and slung it around her neck. She had no pockets so she carried the keys in her mouth. She carried the strapless watch around her neck with a string she had woven out of the blanket fibers.

It was time to leave. She crawled as silently

as possible to the edge of the bed and looked out into the ward. No motion to be seen. The rhythmic snorings wafted down the ward towards her. She slipped over the side and scuttled toward the rear entrance, and poked her head out the opening. Empty, just as she thought. She scuttled out and moved as fast as she could.

She had been preparing her escape by doing push-ups at every free moment to build up her arms. She knew the journey to the surface would be long, even though she would be taking a corridor not known to the general members. In her high position in the Coven of the Dark Dream she had been made privy to many of the alterations and secrets of the cavern that most of the others did not know about.

She moved quickly now and encountered no one, just as she had expected, until she reached a small vestibule carved out of the wall just next to the huge cavern where the ceremony was progressing. Her hands were bloody and her stump hurt terribly.

She sat back against the stone wall and took a minute to catch her breath.

The chanting of the seven hundred present shook the very walls of the cave. In a minute would come the hard part. The vestibule opened out into the cavern about fifty feet from the cave's reception chamber, where there were sure to be guards. She would have to bide her time, and when the time seemed right, when all eyes were focused on the stage and Dwight, she would scramble to the lobby cavern and then use the desk there to hide. Then, again, get out of there when the keepers were watching the ceremony.

Rested now, she leaned forward and peeked into the dimly lit main cavern. The Coven was in full ceremonial dance now, building and building towards a euphoric bliss that Anna knew so well. While in that state there would be nothing in their minds but the ritual, they would be mesmerized and her movements behind them and through weak candlelight thrown by each of the sub-Coven groupings. The cavern floor had been reworked by Bork into tiers horizontal to the stage and descending toward it. On each tier seven areas were marked by white marble pentagrams and each sub-Coven contained thirteen members, all with hooded black robes.

Now they all held candles and as the chant rose in deafening volume, each of the sub-Covens began moving in a circle around the pentagram.

Anna risked a look down to the altar area and there was Dwight, fully garbed in a silken red robe with a thick gold silk rope tied around his waist. Thirteen green-robed acolytes danced in a circle at the altar. Lady Eva stood behind them, her back to the Coven, her hands raised in supplication to the Satanic Image of the Unholy Father of Lies carved out of the limestone back wall of the altar.

On the carved outstretched cupped taloned

hands of the Beast, Anna's baby son lay, still alive, wriggling in a black swaddling cloth.

Anna grimaced at the sight. *Forgive me, little one,* she thought, *but I can't save us both. And your bastard father must be punished for this.* Tears rolled down her cheeks, and she watched the thirteen acolytes throw off their robes and dance skyclad around the flame, then they stopped and knelt down on all fours in sexual supplication to Dwight. Dwight loosed his robe and knelt down behind the closest and entered her briefly from the rear as she screamed, then moved over to the next, and would do so all around the circle. Thus all thirteen women would be sworn to him. Anna knew that after he was done with them, a cadre of thirteen males would dance before the Beast and be bound to Dwight in the same manner.

"I hope you all get AIDS," she mouthed, then made her move into the darkened area, scrambling fifty feet toward the entrance to the reception area, and the guards. When she was five feet from the entrance, a guard, dressed in an orange silk dress robe walked out.

Anna rolled back against a wall, knowing that if he looked her way he would see her. She felt her heart pounding in her chest, as the guard began to turn his head towards her, but then he walked forward to observe Dwight sodomizing the female acolytes. And the noise was so deafening that it would block out the sounds of her movements, so she scrambled, always keeping her eye on the guard. She made it and scurried through the entrance and then rolled behind a desk that sat there. Just then someone entered from the outside. She saw a flash of an orange robe and pulled back her head immediately.

"Goddamn it, Sam!" she heard him yell, and risked a peek. The guard moved across the reception area and into the main chamber entrance.

Anna scuttled quickly behind him and to the smallest exit and zipped through it, stopping right at the entrance to reconnoiter. It was clear, and she scrambled out into the dirt and disappeared into the darkness toward the parking area.

Sharp rocks and sticks cut and stung her palms, and hurt her stump as she crawled, but she took the pain in her exhilaration that she had made it free. It was easy going in a way, because there was plenty of cover. She knew where she was going, and moved from bush to rock in the darkness toward the cave attendants' parking area. She knew that all she had to look out for was the jeep patrol.

In five minutes she found Langdon's polka-dotted monstrosity. She pulled his keys out of her mouth and found the door key. It opened with a seemingly loud click in the darkness. She opened the door and quickly crawled in, cursing the damn overhead light that came on and went out with the opening and closing of the door. If anyone was looking this way, she was burned. Her heart thudded in her chest as she sat back and took a deep breath. It smelled of pungent

123

auto air-freshener. Her hands were slick with blood. She wiped them on her skirt, and fought to control her breathing. "Halfway there," she said out loud. "Halfway."

A feeling of pride filled her. She had done the impossible, escaped from the caverns. Now, let's see if she could escape from the Coven.

The parking lot fell down and away from the cavern following the slope of the hill and thus gave her a good view of the parking area. She searched for the jeep, and finally saw its dark shape down in the moonlit meadow, cruising away from the main lot entrance.

Anna wasn't fooled. There would be guards down there too. In the woods. But in her capacity as High Priestess of the Coven, before her fall, she had been shown a way through the trees, that was wide enough to drive a car. The guards were supposed to have enough time to be able to pick any pedestrian off before he got to the caverns. But Anna wasn't a pedestrian. She had a car and the jeep was headed away from where she was going. She would go to their backs.

She pulled her accelerator extension off her back and practiced finding the pedals with it. She turned suddenly and ripped at the dome-light cover with her bloody fingers until it came off, then she tore the lamp out. If she had to get out of the car, she didn't want the lamp giving away her position.

She fumbled the keys into the ignition and

started the car, engaged the gear, and pressed gently on the stick to the accelerator pedal. The car's motion was jerky at first, but she got the hang of it and guided the car out into the lane. She pressed the brake pedal, the stick slid off, for a moment she thought she was going to hit another car.

The brakes! Shit! Brake lights. She hadn't thought of that before. She stopped the car abruptly with the emergency brake and got out of the car, and using her stick, busted out the brake lights. She hoped no one heard the noise. She crawled back to the car and started forward, heading to the side of the lot and out of it into the relatively smooth meadow. Thank god for the moonlight. She guided the car straight for the forest and through a weaving pattern of trees. It seemed to take forever, but within minutes she reached and mounted a berm and was on the highway that led down the mountain, and to freedom. She accelerated, still driving without headlights until she was several miles down the mountain road.

"All right!" she screamed. "All right, you bastard!"

She was going to get away. She checked the fuel tank. Half a tank. That would get her well into L.A. County, and then she could make a phone call, and be picked up by those who would help her.

She knew just who that would be.

Within twenty minutes she reached the base

of the mountain and drove out onto a major road. She checked her watch. Almost midnight, almost the time her baby would be murdered by his father, and almost the time when Lady Eva would return from her Transition, and know without being told that Anna Kleiber had escaped.

Twelve

KAY TO HENNINGTON

"You've been briefed," said Steve, "but I wanted to tell you a few things more."

Kay cocked her head and listened carefully. They were standing in the parking garage in the safe area where the company special cars were kept. It was six in the morning, and instead of Ken Anderson, Steve himself had come down to give her a send-off. "Remember, Ken's your control. You check in at least twice a day. When you get to Hennington you give Ken a call and let him know you're in place. This Floyd Carlson has a record, but he's only been convicted for minor stuff, but it doesn't mean that he's not capable of a major move if you've nosed your way into something where he's dirty."

She watched Steve move uncharacteristically slowly to a beat-up 1970 red and rust-colored VW bug. He fished into his pocket and pulled out keys on a ring and held them out. She stepped over to him and took the keys. "You look tired," she said, not knowing if she was out of place in doing so.

"No, not tired," he said. "Wary." He grinned at her for a moment, then said, "It is not that I don't trust you. You wouldn't be going if I didn't think you had the skill. But anybody . . . and I do mean anybody, can get found out, and the whole thing can turn bad real fast."

"I understand. But I've cooked up a good cover story: girl with no family, running from an old boyfriend, looking for a quiet, secluded place to live. Don't like to talk about my past too much. I tell him I like Hennington. It would be nice to feel I have a friend in the town, et cetera, et cetera."

Steve smiled. "Okay. Good enough. You look dressed for the part."

Kay had chosen a pair of tight blue jeans that emphasized her choice, aerobically maintained butt, and a tight thin sweater at which, she noticed, even Steve couldn't stop glancing. Not that she had a great chest, she thought, but she did know how to emphasize what she had.

"Hand me the file," Steve said.

"Oh, yes." Kay felt awkward that she had forgotten to give it to him upstairs. She thrust the grey file folder at Steve. It was a dossier on Floyd Carlson and what Steve had been able to learn about him so far. "Wouldn't do to get caught with that, would it?"

"Hardly," said Steve. He took the file and

placed it under his arm, then nodded towards her Fiat. "That'll be safe here. Is that your only bag?"

Kay said, "Yes," and watched Steve as he strode quickly over to her car, picked up the giant blue suitcase and returned to the bug. She unlocked the door quickly and opened it. Steve reached in, worked the latch on the seat and folded it forward and crammed the suitcase into the back seat. "Good luck getting it out when you get up there." He stepped back and Kay pulled the seat to an upright position, tossed her purse on the passenger's seat, and slipped behind the wheel.

Steve closed the door firmly, and she rolled down the window. "Any last words of advice?" She smiled.

"Yeah. Become a librarian. It's safer." He tapped the top of the car and stepped away as she turned the ignition switch. The car purred to life.

"Oh, yeah," Steve said. "There is one last thing. I had Dick change the oil out for some dirty oil, so you can go in for an oil change at Carlson's gas station . . ."

Kay felt a twinge in her mind. Had he doubted her ability to plan a way to get to Floyd.

" . . . that is, if you want to approach him that way?"

"Well, it's the way I was going to make contact with him. I was going to play the dumb blonde about cars, so I didn't think it mattered what shape the oil was in. From reading his file, I guarantee he'll tell me it's dirty even if it isn't."

"Good thinking," said Steve. "Great minds run in the same oil pan, I guess."

Kay had no idea what he was talking about, but she guessed it was a joke and laughed. It seemed to be the right thing to do because Steve laughed back. *Men and their jokes,* she thought. But with Steve it was okay, because he was such a hunk.

She backed the bug out of the stall and flipped Steve a parting wave and putt-putted out of the garage, turned left and headed toward the freeway, and Hennington.

For a moment Steve stood in the exhaust fumes of the VW and looked at the open, empty garage entrance. Early dawn light reflected a slippery red sheen off the pavement that fed out onto the street. Steve stared at it for a moment, then glanced at Kay's red Alfa Romeo. "You be careful," he said out loud to the already-departed Kay in the same tone that he had wanted to say it to her before she left, but hadn't because it would sound too patronizing, though he didn't mean it that way. He just wanted her to be back already, safe and sound, having been successful at her job. It's the same feeling he always felt when he sent one of his people out on a job that he sensed might not be safe.

The early morning traffic moved at a steady pace as Kay headed for the 405 interchange. Once she reached that, she would drive north and then traffic would be minimal since she would be going against the ever-increasing free-way jam that marred every commuter's morning who worked in Los Angeles.

Feelings of excitement swirled inside her. This was her first real class-A case, and all the amorphous possibilities of danger and adventure raced through her mind. Even Steve Brogan himself had come down for the send-off. Not for the first time, she wondered if he had any non-business interest in her. He didn't show it. If he did, but then she was new there, and maybe he didn't want to scare her off.

Kay drove on and within thirty minutes she changed from the 405 to I-5 and was free of the city, cruising along north up towards the mountain range that separates the coast from the enormous central valley of California. She checked her map, and estimated another thirty minutes before her exit. She would get some breakfast there, she decided. She hadn't eaten before she left home. She had been too excited to eat this morning, but now she was ravenous.

The image of a nice scrambled-egg breakfast

reappeared with more frequency as time passed and when she reached the exit, Krasi Road, her mouth was watering. As she cruised to the bottom of the ramp and looked left and right to make a left turn, there were no restaurants, gas stations, Seven-Elevens to be seen. Only open fields running off towards towering mountains in the distance.

"Shit!" she said. "I'm starving!" It had never occurred to her that the road to Hennington would be bare of what had become the blight of the twentieth century, fast-food restaurants.

She made her left, drove a few miles and stopped the car and got out for a stretch, got back in and headed toward the mountains. Within ten minutes she reached another turn, Adina Road, a turny, twisty two-lane highway that led forbiddingly up into the mountains. Clouds hung low and gave the peaks a dark, ominous green tint.

Well, they have to have restaurants in Hennington, she thought, and then it occurred to her that she had never felt this way before. She'd been deprived of breakfast before, due to circumstances, but damn it she was obsessing on this. Her stomach felt like there was a hungry wolf inside her gnawing on her stomach. Why the hell was she feeling this way? It wasn't normal.

She made the turn and looked ahead at the twisty road and wondered if the bug would make it. Steve had assured her earlier that all the cars in the motor pool were finely maintained, but Kay remembered as a child when on trips with her parents how the VW bugs were always chug-chug-chugging the hills, slowing down traffic.

Well, at least there won't be any traffic, she thought as the bug reached the first big grade, and sure enough began its straining chug-chug up the hill.

Soon pine trees began, scraggly dots on the landscape, and within another thousand-foot elevation, Kay was surrounded on either side by a thick, dark forest of pines. The redolent smell of the trees filled her nose, and she wondered with a smile if it was possible to eat tree bark.

The first sign of civilization was a plain board sign that read: HENNINGTON 7 in fading black letters. Five minutes later she spotted an A-frame house in a clearing and soon there were small cabins and private dirt roads every hundred yards.

She passed a large rock and followed the curve of the road around and finally broke out into a small main street. She passed a gas station, a small general store, the police station and library, and spotted a restaurant and pulled abruptly in, got out and moved toward the door with a purpose. She practically yanked the door off its hinges in opening it, and made right for the counter, the fastest place to get served.

What is the matter with me? she thought.

"I'll have a ham-and-cheese omelette," she

said to the waitress, an elderly woman dressed in a red-and-pink plaid shift who had her back to Kay.

They did not acknowledge Kay. She patiently continued to do whatever she was doing. Kay couldn't see, because the woman's body blocked her view.

"I'll have . . ."

"I heard you," said the woman without turning around.

Kay picked up the warning rattle in the old woman's voice, sat back, and for the first time looked around. The place was packed with morning traffic even though there hadn't been many cars in the parking lot. And every person in the place was staring at her, even those with their backs to her had turned in a straining twist. Some had turned completely around.

And the place was filled with a dead silence. *Oh shit. oh shit, oh shit.*

"I'm sorry," she said to everyone, looking around the room. "I haven't eaten in three days, and I'm very hungry."

This had no effect on the people. They continued to stare. Suddenly, the waitress turned around and Kay sat up straight in shock. Though the woman had naturally white arms and hands, her facial skin was a smooth black. Her features were Negroid, a wide nose and thick lips, and if it hadn't been for her cloudy starred eyes, Kay would have considered her an attractive woman. Her white hair formed a corona that off-

134

set the black of her round face, and made her eyes jump out of a dark pit.

"You from outta town?" the woman asked, and the restaurant burst into that special laughter that people who know each other seem to have at an inside joke. Soon the noise died down and the people gradually began returning to eating their meal.

The waitress put a glass of water in front of Kay, and reached for the coffee pot. Kay pushed her cup forward, and the waitress poured.

"Thank you," Kay said, not looking into those strange eyes. She was surprised that the woman began talking to her in a civil voice. "This place always makes outsiders mad with hunger. Where you from?"

"Los Angeles." Kay looked at her briefly, and the starred eyes didn't scare her as bad. She wondered for a moment if the woman was blind, but that was stupid, how could she pour a cup of coffee like that, if she were?

"Angelenos always get the hungriest," she said. "Enjoy your breakfast." She moved off with the coffeepot, filling other needy cups as she went, and teasing the locals good naturedly.

Minutes later the waitress set before her a ham-and-cheese omelette with hashed brown potatoes and white toast on the side.

Kay devoured the meal, got the bill, left enough money for the food and a tip on the counter and walked out into the early morning grey. She belched.

"Jesus, what's wrong with me?" she said out loud. She felt fine now, stuffed with food. She hadn't eaten a big breakfast since she'd turned sixteen and wanted to fit in her prom gown.

She checked her watch. Eight-thirty. Too early, she decided. I don't want to look too eager. Maybe I'd be better off finding a motel room first.

She got to her car just as a light drizzle began to fall. She slipped behind the wheel and drove the rest of main street. No hotels, no motels. A grain shop, a hardware store and a few other assorted restaurants, but that was it.

She stopped at a pay phone and checked the yellow pages. No hotels, no motels, for real, in the whole of town. It wasn't that small, she thought. She found a newspaper stand and bought a copy of *The Watch*, the town's only print organ, and looked under rooms to rent. Nothing.

She threw the paper on the seat next to her and scowled. She hadn't expected this. She thought for a moment, then smiled to herself. Maybe she could use this to her advantage.

She started up the car and headed back down main street towards the only garage in town— that had to be Floyd Carlson's Chevron station.

"I want to speak to Floyd Carlson," Kay told the beefy young mechanic standing in the garage bay.

136

"He's busy," said the mechanic. The name "Bob" was embroidered on his work shirt in dark blue thread. "I can help you."

"I want the owner, " she insisted, and Bob's eyes went flinty, his mouth forming a small O.

He turned on his heels and went to a door and knocked, then opened it, and said in a loud voice, "Floyd, there's a lady out here, who can't talk to the hired help. She wants the *Oh*-ner."

"What the fuck?" she heard a man say. His voice was a high warble.

Bob stepped out of the way, and a small man, a head shorter than Kay, strode out of the office, looking fiercely agitated. His eyes, no kidding, were shit brown in color, and moved around in his head like they had a mind of their own. Finally they fixed on Kay.

Kay's heart rate began to trip-hammer in her chest. Man, if looks could kill, this guy was an assassin. He stared at her for a few seconds more, and then gradually his angry expression began to fade from his face, like his sanity had been restored. Finally, he smiled pleasantly and took a few steps towards her.

"Can I he'p you?" he said in a fawning voice. Now his gaze flicked up and down her sweater, took in a panorama of her chest, and finally zipped down to her crotch, resting finally on her face.

"I'm sorry to bother you, Mr. Carlson."

"No bother for such a pretty lady," he said, squinting his eyes.

"Thank you," she demurred, feigning embarrassment, but thinking, *Boy, this guy is too much. Look at that noggin.* His head looked about the size of a large cantaloupe, with dark brown hair slicked back with Brylcreme and old gob grease.

She pulled down on her sweater to show a little nervousness, and watched his eyes feast on her cleavage. She knew what this guy was about, no questions asked. She said, "My dad, always said to ask for the owner, 'cause you would get better service. I didn't know that you were busy. I'm really sorry."

For a moment, she thought that she might have laid it on too thick, because Floyd said nothing at first. After what seemed like a long time, he grinned, and put out his hand. "Call me Floyd. I'm the owner. And your daddy was right. I'm gonna service you good."

"I'm Kay." She took his hand and found his hands were surprisingly large and very strong.

"That your VW over there?"

"That's it." They walked together over to the car. He took the keys she offered him, opened the door and got in the car.

"Noticed the suitcase," he said. "Where you headed?"

"Looking around for some place like this. Where asshole ex-boyfriends aren't allowed."

"He hit ya, huh?"

"Bad. He's a maniac."

"No excuse for hitting a woman. Man oughtta be castrated."

"I'd do it myself, but he's not worth going to jail over."

"Didn't you go to your family? Your dad, or brother?"

"My whole family's dead. I was an only child. We moved around a lot. Don't have any relatives that I know about. Got nobody, really." She bowed her head and tried to look like she was going to cry.

"That is tough, Kay," Floyd said. He turned the ignition key, and the engine putted to life. He revved up the engine and made a show of listening. He revved it again. Again and really punched it, until the noise was deafening, then backed off. Listened intently like he was divining some truth. He shut it off. "It's a good thing you brought it in, Kay."

"Oh, jeez, I just brought it in for an oil change. Is there something wrong with it? Is it going to cost a lot? I don't have much money."

"Don't worry about it. Not gonna rip you off. You can do some filin' for me or something to make up the difference of what you got."

"No, that's okay," she said instinctively, giving him a wary look.

Floyd's voice register was so high that his chortle sounded like notes from a flute. "I'm not hittin' on you, girl. Nothin' like that, I'm telling you."

Kay affected a little hesitation in her voice.

"You're sure? 'Cause . . . 'cause, I'm not like that, the way some women are."

"Sure, I'm sure. Hell, I got a sister that you remind me of. I'm trying to show you that all men aren't like that asshole boyfriend you're running from. And even if he did find you here, I'd smear him. Can't stand woman beaters."

Floyd got out of the car, and closed the door.

Kay did her best to seem embarrassed, but gratefully so. She looked around at the high mountains, the clouds, trees, and then hesitating only briefly she said, "Well the pines sure make the air smell sweet around here. And I don't think he'd find me here . . . but I looked around this morning and there are no motels, no rooms to rent . . . I don't know where I'll stay . . ."

"Got just the thing for you," Floyd said. "The Cabins. A friend of mine owns them, and I can get you in."

"Sounds expensive," she said, looking him directly into those shit brown eyes.

"Naw. Don't worry about it, I'm tellin' you. People around here are glad to help any female who's been done wrong by her man. There are a lot of people up here with good hearts, believe you me. I'll put the word out you're looking for a job and you'll pay the people back when you're back on your feet."

"Sounds too good to be true."

"Which usually means it is," Floyd completed the saying for her, sounding insulted. "But, it's

140

your choice. Nobody's forcing you." He handed her back her keys, and started to turn.

"I'm sorry," Kay said. She reached out and touched his arm and fought down a shocked reaction. Touching his arm was like touching an electric cable. The muscles of his thin, sinewy arm, seemed to vibrate with a nervous energy.

She let go and looked at him. He was smiling.

"That's okay," he said. "A girl can't be too careful. But she's got to be able to tell when a person's sincere or not, too. I can tell, you've got a lot to learn about nice people, Kay."

"Yeah, I guess so," she said.

"Now, I'll go make some phone calls and you wait here. Leave the keys in the car." Floyd disappeared into his office and Kay sauntered back to the bug, opened the door and sat down. She slipped the keys in the car and turned on the radio and fiddled with the tuner until she picked up a station. Bakersfield, most likely, she was too out of range for any L.A. station.

Well, I've done it, she thought. Now I've got to get to a phone and check in as soon as I get settled. And she'd better tell them that she'd check in once a day instead of twice unless something special came up, because if she got caught making a long-distance telephone call, the question would come up who was she calling if she had no relatives.

She thought for a moment, then felt a little

141

relieved. She could tell them that she was harassing her ex-boyfriend. That would work.

Kay looked up and saw Floyd coming towards her. "Got good news for you. Lana and Jane are coming for you from The Cabins. They've got room for you and you've got a job starting tomorrow at Mama Cabali's Restaurant. She says she even knows you. Remembered you from breakfast."

"Oh, great," Kay said. She was going to work for that woman? Boy, undercover work really did have its twists and turns.

Floyd went back into the office and ten minutes later a 1988 green Chevy turned into the station and two young girls, eighteen or nineteen, with blond hair and blue eyes got out and walked right up to her. "Hi, Kay," they said like they had known her all their lives.

"Hi," she said back.

"I'm Lana," said the one with the sharp chin, "and she's Jane."

Jane had already moved around Kay and got Kay's bag out of the VW. "Ready to go?"

"Yes. I want to thank Floyd . . ."

"He's busy," said Lana. "He'll see you tonight and you can thank him then. Believe me, he's a nice guy, but when he's interrupted, boy he can be a bear."

"Yeah," Kay said. "I found out a little while ago."

After putting the bag in the trunk, Lana shuttled her into the passenger side of the front seat.

Jane slipped in directly behind her. Lana started the car and turned onto Main Street and back out of town. In a short time, Lana guided the car onto a dirt road that disappeared into the forest. The road was smooth with wear and only slightly muddy from the light drizzle earlier in the morning. They emerged from the forest into a clearing and headed up toward a clump of trees and other parked cars.

"Where are the cabins?" asked Kay.

"The what?" Lana said.

"The cabins. Floyd said you had room for me at The Cabins."

Jane snickered in back, and Lana laughed outright.

"What?" Kay was mystified.

"It's *Floyd*. He's a card. He mispronounces it. It's the caverns. We've got room for you at the caverns."

"Oh," said Kay. A sinking feeling passed through her mind. She looked off to her left. A jeep with two men carrying assault rifles was approaching. "Those men have guns," she said.

"Guards," said Lana. "They protect us."

"I think I wanna go back," Kay said.

"There's no going back," said Lana.

"You're ours," Jane said in a raspy voice, and then Kay heard the metallic click of a gun being cocked. "Don't turn around."

Kay fought the fear, but couldn't help it. She felt warm urine release and it soaked her jeans. Lana guided the car up to the group of trees and rocks and parked in a clear spot. The men leapt out of the jeep and opened the door and pulled her out of the car and slammed her against the car. One man patted her down for weapons, bitching about the pee on his hand. Everyone else laughed as she was led through a clump of trees and into the cavern, and the unknown.

Kay felt guilt and shame warring in her mind. She'd gotten snagged not an hour into the town. One of the guards cuffed her hands behind her back and then marched her between some trees and into a cave opening. She was taken through a side tunnel that ran along what appeared to be a terraced auditorium and then down behind it, then back into a labyrinth of corridors until they came to two main tunnels.

"Go down this one," he said, pointing to the right. "At the end is Lady Eva. When you come to her, kneel, and say, 'Have mercy, O My Lady,' and maybe she will."

Kay hesitated, and the guard said matter-of-factly, "I'm just trying to be nice. She already knows you're here, and if she has to send Cutter or Radd to get you, you aren't gonna like it here, at all."

He turned away as if it were a foregone conclusion that she would go down, and because of that Kay started down the corridor. It twisted and turned and narrowed, and in a few minutes she came out into a large, well-lit cavern complete with bedroom furniture and a sofa and chair and table. The walls were draped with black silk material. And sitting on a stool in front of a dressing table and mirror sat a strikingly beautiful woman with raven black hair.

Kay forgot exactly what she was supposed to say but said, "My Lady, I am honored," and hoped it would do.

The woman rose and fixed her eyes upon Kay. "I want you to tell me everything about yourself."

Kay felt drawn into the woman's eyes, and fought the feeling. She had to keep her mouth shut. "I'm up here looking for a job and now I'm in this mess, and I did not do anything. And that's the truth."

The woman pointed a finger at her, studying her as if to burn Kay's image into her memory. "You are lying to me, and you will tell me the truth, you can be sure of that."

Kiss my ass, thought Kay.

"No," said the woman. "But you will kiss mine, and then you will tell what you know."

"Shit!" Kay said. "Are you a mind reader or something like that?" She was stalling for time while she figured something out, and not doing a very good job of it she had to admit.

"Something like that. I have my good days and I have my bad days. And today is one of my good days." She never took her eyes off

Kay, and called over her shoulder, "Cutter! Radd! It's playtime."

And when the things came ambling in with their horrid fanged faces, and full erections, she said hurriedly, "I take it back. I'll tell you everything, just get those things away from me."

And in the end when she had told all, Lady Eva let them have her anyway. "But don't kill her," she cautioned. "I have a specific use for her. And if she's not whole when you're done, I'll kill you both."

With this she left the chamber, and Kay screamed and screamed.

Later in the day Floyd sat in his office drinking a cup of coffee out of a joke mug that was shaped like a woman's tit. He picked it up and drank out of the nipple. He removed it from his lips, and said, "Thank you, Kay," to it.

She had saved him a lot of trouble. As the Procurer for the Coven, Floyd had been responsible for many new acolytes, but recently, unknown to anyone but himself, Lady Eva had given him an assignment to find a woman just like Kay. Same build, mostly, and he had been nervous that he wouldn't find one quick enough, and here one is delivered to him. No family. No one knowing where she was. Perfect.

He laughed and took another sip from the tit mug. *I'm gonna see if Lady Eva'll let me screw her,* he thought. *No harm in asking.*

He sat for a moment and what briefly came into his head was a bit of social reasoning that often escaped him. He decided against asking her, because Lady Eva had wanted a woman like her so much that there must be some good reason, and it would be stupid to piss off Lady Eva. That's what had happened to Anna Kleiber, now look what happened to her. Now that she'd escaped, she'd really get sat on hard.

Floyd had no doubt that they would find her, and that punishment would be meted out. Yes. Lady Eva was that powerful, and that merciless.

Why, this morning everybody in the Coven received a little piece of The Keeper's body for breakfast and a big chunk of the guards who were on duty were handed out to key personnel, to remind them how important their duties were to safety of the Coven.

And after stopping by the station to thank him for the female acquisition, Lady Eva herself had gone out on the hunt for Anna Kleiber, and no one hunted better than Lady Eva, no one on Earth.

Thirteen

BARUCH KATZMER

Steve realized that he had driven near the museum in Pasadena a thousand times and never knew it.

He missed the driveway at first, catching a glimpse of a small bronze sign affixed to the flush greystone wall that encircled the estate as he zipped by.

The museum was situated in the now-declining affluent area of Pasadena, back off the road hidden by olive and eucalyptus trees. Land of rich homes and finely manicured lawns, it was as if someone had deliberately hidden the museum grounds away behind a veil of trees and shrubs so that no one could find it.

He turned around and made a left and followed a drive through the arching bows of elm trees. The property was deceptive. Entering upon a normal drive, the amount of area covering the museum drive opened up like a slice of pie; where he had entered had been the sharp point.

Steve estimated the land to cover thirty acres, in the middle of which stood a massive reproduction of a seventeenth-century gothic cathedral, complete with the characteristic arches, flying buttresses, and a central steeple.

Steve cruised up to the near-empty parking area and parked. He got out and stood with his hands on his hips, admiring the building. The central of three portals had a giant rose window over it, and though Steve was no expert in architecture, it seemed that whoever had built this had been a stickler for minute detail. It looked exactly like the cathedrals he had seen in France.

He checked his watch. It read one-fifteen. He was fifteen minutes early. He walked the manicured, red-brick walk up to the central portal and couldn't resist a glance up at the two bell towers over the left and right portals. There was a balcony between the two located directly over the giant rose window. Once he talked with Dr. Katzmer he thought it might be nice to stand there and see what kind of view of the city it offered.

He entered through the center door and was immediately struck by the cool air of the cathedral. A young docent sat at a mahogany desk and looked up from her book, as if surprised someone had actually come to see the collection.

"Hi," said Steve. "I have an appointment with Dr. Katzmer."

She pointed toward the left. "Go over there where the ambulatory begins. There's a door. Administration. Mrs. Nabov." She smiled.

"USC, right?"

"How did you know?"

"All the best-looking women go there?"

Big smile. "Thank you."

"Don't mention it," Steve said and stepped over to administration.

Mrs. Nabov was an elderly woman with a Slavic accent. Hearing that Steve had an appointment with Dr. Katzmer, she pointed to a set of stairs just past her door. "Excuse me for not going up with you, but my arthritis. Oh, it hurts."

"Of course," said Steve. "I hope you feel better."

The woman nodded appreciation, and said, "Just go up. Follow the arrows. And don't waste your time knocking. He could be anywhere up there and never hear you. Just walk in."

"I'm a little early."

"Time means nothing to that man—nothing!" She held her left hand out like a signal to stop. She shook her head in good-natured disgust.

Steve laughed to himself after he left the office. He found the stairs easily enough. They were the kind that switch back and forth until you got to the landing. He seemed to switch back and forth forever, until he came upon a

150

long narrow hall that ran along the uppermost arches of the nave. A small brass sign read *Curator* and an arrow pointed to a narrow set of stairs that disappeared into the walkway's wall.

Steve was forced to duck as he entered the narrow stairway, and as he ascended he was reminded that this building was of another time, when the average man was five-foot-six, not his twentieth-century, Wheaties and steak-fed, six-foot-four-inch frame.

His shoulders missed the walls of the stairway by less than an inch on each side as he ascended the stairs. They gave out on a narrow landing that preceded a seven-foot arch. He strode through the arch and entered an antechamber, the north wall of which was an arched doorway, filled with heavy black oak double doors. Steve felt as if he had traveled back in time—instead of a doorknob, heavy cast-iron rings and levers stood in place.

Even though the woman had told him to go right in, he felt uncomfortable entering someone's office without knocking, so he assuaged his discomfort by rapping lightly on the door as he pushed the door open.

He stepped through the portal and closed the door behind him, stifling an audible gasp as he did so. He was standing in the "attic" of the old cathedral, that portion of the ancient building over the main body of the church. The room ran the full one hundred and fifty feet and the roof peaked thirty feet above his head. Dazzling colored light filtered through the stained glass rose windows in slanted shafts onto the clutter that filled the room. Dust motes caught in the shafts of light danced and moved gracefully in swirls.

Steve saw no one in evidence and stepped forward, casting a fascinated glance at the display cases stored up here, and the many dioramas depicting various rituals from ancient Egypt to African voodoo to modern American witchcraft. The room had a dried, dusty savor to it, that spoke of true antiquity. He took his time walking toward the center of the room where the debris of the collection cleared, and he found himself standing under the central spire of the cathedral, where the attic intersected with its west and east wings. Steve glanced quickly down each, and saw more shafts of multicolored light playing with dust motes around collection display cases and diorama figures.

He thought to call out, but listening carefully he thought he heard music coming from straight ahead, so he continued forward. His initial uneasiness had dwindled and now his curiosity was rising. He glided past two display cases filled with shrunken heads and stopped before a life-sized diorama stored precariously atop a number of three-foot-high crates. It depicted black-hooded druids standing around a fire, holding a small wicker basket on a long pole just above the imagined lick of the flames. In the small basket lay a lifelike naked baby mannequin.

Steve grimaced and walked around the display.

He found the source of the music and the curator at the same time. The plaintive sounds of Billie Holiday's rendition of "Lady Sings the Blues" blared from a battered radio/cassette player that sat on a large wooden worktable. The curator sat hunched over an immense drafting table, examining something. Steve caught a glimpse of a grizzled black beard and fine gold antique glasses, something he would have expected of an older man. Yet, the curator could not be more than four or five years older than Steve. *Forty-three, max* thought Steve.

"Excuse me," Steve said loud enough to be heard over the blaring cassette player.

Baruch Katzmer covered what he was examining and swung full around facing Steve. "What do you want?" he said, a look of accusation on his face.

Steve felt unsure of himself. He said simply, "I'm your two-thirty appointment, Dr. Katzmer."

Katzmer blinked large doe eyes at him, and as if clearing cobwebs from his memory with each blink. He smiled and extended his hand. "Yes, of course. I apologize . . . sort of the absent-minded professor at times, my wife says."

"No need to apologize. You were absorbed in your work."

"Sometimes my work is not appreciated, take the druids for example . . ." Katzmer pointed to the diorama behind Steve. "It took me months to conceive and build that, and the board of directors refused to let me show it without remov-

153

ing the baby from the wicker basket. Too grue-some, they said. I said I wasn't going to display it at all if it wasn't authentic, so it sits up here . . ." His voice trailed off and he made a few *tsk, tsk* sounds, then pointed toward a desk chair sitting all by itself near the drafting board. "Have a seat and tell me what it is I can help you with, Mr. . . ." he searched for the name . . . "oh, God, my mind is slipping."

"Steve Brogan," Steve said as he settled down into the desk chair. It was surprisingly comfort-able, and as he looked over into Dr. Katzmer's face he felt an unexplainable liking for the man.

Steve reached inside his coat and pulled out the glassine baggie holding the medallion from the graveyard. He handed it over to Katzmer, who gently placed it on his examination table.

He reached over and pulled a black silk cloth-covered board—like a jeweler would use—from a stack of such boards. He lifted the glassine bag, spread it open and gently let the medallion slide onto the black cloth. "Oh," he said to him-self, as if oblivious to Steve being in the room. He reached for forceps and tweezers and gently discarded the bag and began to manipulate the coin, first flipping it and then turning it, and with such delicacy that Steve rather thought Dr. Katzmer was fondling it.

Katzmer laid the coin down and put a jew-eler's eyepiece to his eye and bent over the me-dallion again. Again he said to himself, "Oh."

Steve scooted his chair closer.

"There's writing . . . minute writing. It's almost surely original," he said to Steve. "Of course you know that, right?"

"I brought it to you to identify it, Dr. Katzmer."

"Call me Katz, please." He gestured toward the coin with a twitch of his eye. "You bring me this, and you can call me Katz, believe me."

"Tell me what I brought you, Katz."

Steve saw Katzmer struggling to pull his eyes away from the coin, unable to manage it. He spoke through the side of his mouth. "You brought me one of the three coins of the *Das Fayden*—at least that's what it appears to be. "Where did you find it? Near a grave, or a funeral site of some kind?"

"On the headstone related to a case I'm working on."

"Is this the only coin you've found?"

"Yes."

"Hm-m-m. Let us hope that it's the first."

"Why is that?"

For the first time Katzmer pulled his eyes away from the coin and stared straight into Steve's eyes. "Because, if it's the first coin used then there is more time before something horrible happens.

"But we'll talk about that later. What I want to know is if you are a believer in the supernatural? It's important, so think about the question carefully."

Steve saw that the curator was serious and so

Steve did take a moment to reflect. Finally he said, "No. Not really. I believe in instincts and that's about it."

"Well, you are going to have to use your instincts when you listen to me and decide whether you trust me and my judgment. Because I *do* believe in the supernatural. Not when I first started out. When I first began I set out to debunk it. I found the study interesting as a reflection of the common hysteria of the human mind. I was content with that, but found that there is universal Good and Evil out in the cosmos. And this," he held up the coin, "is part of the fulcrum of the balance of the two forces."

"I don't understand," Steve said, and sat forward. Katzmer didn't appear crazy; his face had taken on the expression of a professor lecturing a student. Steve decided to hear him out. "But tell me everything. I'll listen, and reject nothing out of hand . . . I promise."

Katzmer paused and looked him full in the eye. "Good. Then you are as smart as you look, and if I'm right about this you're going to have to be plenty smart." Katzmer twisted up and pulled the cloth off what he had covered when Steve had introduced himself. With his free hand (his other still holding the coin) he retrieved an ancient-looking leather-bound book the size of a paperback novel. "It's amazing that something this small could be so important. When I found it I expected a big book like you see in the movies, with hinges and a lock on it. But it was like this . . ."

"What book is that?"

"*This,*" said Katzmer with unaffected awe in his voice, "is *Das Fayden*. It is the book of Eternal Darkness and the Book of Eternal Light."

"Sounds like a grade B movie . . ."

"Life *is* a grade B movie," Katzmer said, looking at Steve full in the face for the first time, taking his measure. "Basic good versus basic evil, with all the grey areas in between.

"I was like you once, a disbeliever, a skeptic. A man who found it easier to scoff than to take the time to understand. My whole *scene* was debunking the myth, and I was great at it. Then one day I came upon the trail of *Das Fayden* and all that changed."

Katzmer pulled back from Brogan and wiped the corner of his mouth with the side of his hand. He stared hard at Brogan and brought the ancient book up under Brogan's nose. "Take it," Katzmer said. "Take hold of it, but be careful. I gave up much to get it and broke a number of laws smuggling it into the country."

Brogan took the small book from Katzmer and immediately felt the same disdain that he felt when he handled the medallion—only more intensely, as if rotted, concentrated liquid energy radiated from the book and up into his hands and arms, trying to permeate his whole body.

The brown leather cover itself felt soft and supple.

Steve flicked his gaze to Katzmer and back again to the book. "Anything else I should know?" He opened the book to the first page filled with black runic script on yellow parchment.

"Yes," said Katzmer. "The pages are made of human infant skin—infant no more than two weeks old. The ink is a mixture of minerals and the infant's blood."

Steve thumbed through a few pages until he came to a diagram of three medallions of different sizes like he had given over to Katzmer. "What do these medallions mean?" he asked.

"Well that's the question, isn't it?" said Katzmer. "I've translated only part of the text, and reached the conclusion that I go public with this thing. Next month's issue of *National Anthropologist* is publishing my findings so far, and then I'll have a flood of calls demanding access to *Das Fayden,* and I'll be obliged to acquiesce to a few of them at least. Things like this have to be opened up for examination. They're too important for just one mind to attack. Great as that mind might be." He smiled mischievously at Steve.

"What are we talking here?" Steve asked. "Occult? What kind of occult?"

"The most basic, I'm afraid. I really think someone else can answer your question better than I."

"I really don't want to know much more," said Steve. "I don't like the occult . . ." He would tie up the loose ends, he decided and hand it over to someone else. He had made a promise to Ken and he would keep it unless there was some reason not to. He'd still help Molly with Daphne's father if there was any way he could do that, but then he was out.

"Not so fast, Mr. Brogan." Katzmer turned from him, grabbed a scrap of paper and a pen and scribbled something on it. He handed the paper to Steve.

Steve took it and examined it. It read "Lady May" followed by a phone number. Steve put it in his pocket.

"That woman will have all the answers for you. She is most knowledgeable in this matter."

Steve had made his decision. "I told you I'm going to drop this case . . ."

"It's too late, Mr Brogan. You're already involved . . ."

"What are you talking about?"

"Open to the back cover of the book."

Steve did so. In the inside of the back cover were cut three circular holes.

Katzmer handed him the medallion. "Put it in," he told Steve.

Steve fitted the medallion into the top hole.

"From what I've translated so far, that first medallion is a sign that the Restoration has begun. The text is specific, that all who touch that

159

medallion are inextricably bound in this matter. In short, Steve Brogan, I don't think you have a choice."

"We'll see about that," said Steve. He closed the book and handed it back to Katzmer. "You're going to tell me what the script on the medallion means."

"Leave it with me. I need to study it."

Steve hesitated for a moment. Normally, he would not have allowed it, but something told him he could trust Katzmer. Besides he was going to turn this case over to someone else, anyway. Kathy Fandino, the L.A.P.D. detective. He was getting a bad feeling on this. "Okay, but you're responsible for it."

"Don't worry. I'll take good care of it."

Steve fished around in his pocket and pulled out a business card. He dropped it on the table. "When you translate it please call me right away."

Katzmer smiled at him, that same mischievous smile. "Okay," he said. "One question? Why do you hate the occult so much?"

"In my line of work occult is just another name for crazy. Normally sane people finding reasons for doing insane things."

"Oh," said Katzmer. "There are two forms of magic, y'know. White and Black. You call Lady May. She's as good a human being as there is on this planet, and she's into the occult. She's very special, and she's definitely not insane."

Steve shrugged, turned and walked away.

He showed himself out, with Katzmer's admonition still ringing in his ears: *In short, Steve Brogan. I don't think you've got a choice.*

He tried to wipe it from his mind as he drove away, and finally managed to by pulling out the telephone number Katzmer had given him and dialing it. As it rang and rang, Steve thought that he would make this last contact on the case and then withdraw. He had paid Senator Dest enough as it was, and he would make a play for Molly on his own merits if the opportunity presented itself.

On the seventh ring, when he was just about to hang up, the telephone was answered. "Hello," said the person, in the high sweet tone of Carlotta Chalmers.

Christ, he'd dialed the wrong number. Hadn't he? "May I speak with Lady May, please?" he asked anyway.

"Speaking," she said. "My, you are a good detective, aren't you, Mr. Brogan."

"Explain to me the Lady May title," Steve said.

"But of course, Mr. Brogan. Not now, though. Tonight, I'm giving a party. Eight o'clock. Please come. I will go over everything with you tonight. Agreed?"

Steve hesitated for a moment, and thought of

Molly. Is she part of this? God, he hoped not. "Agreed," he said finally, and hung up the car phone.

Fourteen

THE PARTY

Instead of returning to the office, Steve drove to his home in Woodland Hills. The house was his. The divorce had gone as smooth as it could have gone in terms of property. Constance had come from money, and the breakup hadn't been about who got what, anyway. It had been about trust. And once that was broken, how it could never be the same. Yes, she'd gone back to her "people," as she had called them, and left him his house and his business, and if anyone were to ask him, a broken heart.

Steve checked as he walked in the door. It was three o'clock, and Mrs. Chalmers's party was only five hours away. He wanted to clean up and have time to think. He made himself a turkey sandwich on white bread and sat down at the kitchen table to eat it, washing it down with two big glasses of milk.

He pulled his notebook from his pocket and flipped it up and reviewed his notes on the Chalmers case. He had bad feelings about this now and was seriously considering dropping it, Senator Veronica Dest be damned. But there was the Molly factor to consider, not to mention the girls, Daphne and Penny. And then, of course, he couldn't help wondering why that stiff Thom had to be in the picture.

Steve came across the quick scribble in his notebook that was Thom's license plate number, and he stretched out and plucked the telephone receiver from the kitchen's wall phone. He called Nancy Ellis, a detective friend of his at Winnetka Station and gave her the license plate number and asked her to run it for him when she had time. He thanked her and hung up.

It felt odd to be home in the middle of the day, but Steve knew himself and that tonight would undoubtedly be a late night, so he forced himself to relax. He would nap for an hour and get up and work out with the weights, take a jog, then get cleaned up, go into the office and work late until time for the party. Between now and then he had to decide whether he was to keep his people on this case or not. He hadn't had the crawl like he had on this case since the Balatta Sting, so many years ago. And what was he going to do if Molly was deep into this occult shit?

164

By the time he got into bed, he figured the nap would truly do him good. He fell asleep and was dreaming of small blank medallions that glittered seductively, when he came suddenly awake. He sat up and swung around, putting both feet on the floor—the plush pile of the carpeting seemed to intertwine between his toes. He looked down, and when he looked up Daphne was standing there . . . she reached toward him, her eyes glittering . . . then she disappeared as quickly as she had come.

Steve shook his head and put his hands on the mattress beside him and squeezed it. It was real. "A waking dream," he said to the empty room.

"Daphne! NO!"

Molly rushed fully into the room and over to where Daphne and Penny sat, between them her Sacred Book open to a love enchantment page. The white bone powder had been used to draw a pentagram, north pointed, thank heavens. She picked up the book quickly and blew out the candle that had sat at the head of the spine. "Didn't I tell you *never* to touch this book? Was that Steve Brogan's name I heard you chant?" Molly looked down at the page of incantation. At the top in large script was the title of the spell: *Lascivious Romanticus Vadema.*

"What verse were you at when I interrupted you? Tell me!"

Both girls began to cry. "The first, the first."

Molly let out a sigh of relief. She had broken the incantation just in time.

She calmed the girls down and then asked Daphne, "What did you think you were doing with the spell, honey?"

"I wanted Mr. Brogan to love me . . ."

"Oh, honey, no . . ." Molly sat down on Daphne's bed and held her. Daphne slumped against her side. "There are different kinds of love, Daphne. The reason Mommy tells you not to use my book is not because she doesn't trust you, but because there are a lot of things in the world you're just not old enough to know. You could have hurt Mr. Brogan very much if I hadn't stopped you.

"You're a child . . . you can't use this kind of spell on him . . . not if you really love him . . . you probably would have scared him to death . . ." She looked up at Penny, who was standing by the bed drying her tears. "Even Mommy doesn't use this spell . . . it's not fair. It's taking advantage . . . and when you're a little older, I'll explain that . . ."

Daphne did not look up, but mewled, "Are you still mad at me?"

"No. But I am grounding you, and you, too, Penny-Peanut. This book is not to be tampered with, and you should have told me right away that your sister was playing with it."

166

The girls groaned.

Molly stood up. "Three days, no TV. And this," she held out the book. "Never touch this without permission again." She turned and walked out of the room. She had the party to get ready for, and Steve was coming tonight. She wondered if he had felt anything of Daphne's aborted spell. Probably not. And a good thing, too.

As Steve drove up the drive to Chalmers manor, he had a sinking feeling that he had already made a faux pas. He was pulling in right at eight-thirty and the drive and area surrounding were filled with limousines and Rolls Royces. Mercedes and Cadillacs fleshed out the rest of the lot, twenty-seven cars in all, and a couple he saw walking right up to the door were dressed in a tuxedo and long strapless evening gown.

Steve had regaled himself in California casual. He wore black pants with a camel-hair sports jacket, with a white dress shirt, open at the collar. He had on black socks and black soft-leather loafers.

He was greeted at the door by the huge Motu, who was dressed in a tuxedo. Motu looked him up and down and smiled. "It's a welcome change, Mr. Brogan. I hate these monkey suits myself."

"I'm embarrassed," Steve admitted.

"Don't be. You are welcome in this house," Motu said with solemn sincerity. He stepped aside and let Steve pass. Steve walked in wondering what Motu had meant by that. Before he could ask him, Motu had shut the door and left him to trail behind towards the left as he moved through room to connecting room of the house. Steve followed and when they had gotten to the back part of the house he stood at the threshold of a large area room in the rear that was perfect for entertaining. Here elegantly dressed people were mingling and drinking their drinks and talking their talk.

An elderly man who might or might not be famous sat at a piano playing Gershwin tunes. Motu stopped at the wide entrance and stood straight and announced, "Mr. Steve Brogan," then turned, winked and walked back towards the front of the house.

Steve froze in embarrassment. The room, which was previously filled with conversation, stopped. Now there was a dead silent sea of well-dressed bon vivants staring at him.

From the opposite side of the room, Carlotta Chalmers, dressed in an aqua blue evening gown, her white hair perfectly coifed, separated herself from a small group and waved him forward with an engaging smile. "Come in, come in. Everyone, this is Steve Brogan. Come in, Steve Brogan. Come in."

If Steve thought he had felt embarrassed before, he was mortified now. Absolutely everybody was now staring at him, and the man at the piano stopped playing. Mrs. Chalmers floated over and in a charming manner took his arm and led him into the room and toward a liveried man holding a silver platter filled with champagne glasses. She took two glasses from the tray and handed him one.

The general chitchat began to start up again, and as Steve took the offered glass from Mrs. Chalmers, he spotted Molly. She looked beautiful in a green sequined strapless gown. He felt a yearning in his heart, and the thought that he might not see her again after tonight pained him greatly. Maybe she wasn't part of this occult thing.

Thom stood next to her glaring at him.

Must not like that I took them for pizza, thought Steve.

Mrs. Chalmers turned to the pianist and said, "Bill, play something." The music started immediately, low and background for sure. Muzak couldn't have done better.

"Mrs. Chalmers, give me five minutes with you, and I'll leave you to your friends," said Steve, surprised at himself. As sometimes happened he had reached his decision without knowing it. He would back out of this one, despite his attraction to Molly. Give her as much information as he had collected, suggest the police, bill her of course, and try to reach out for Molly later.

"I know what you're thinking, Steve Brogan,

169

but I must ask you to stay." Carlotta glanced over her shoulder at Thom and Molly. "They make a lovely couple, don't they?" she said dryly.

Steve cast a quick look. Thom was still eyeballing him heavily and Molly looked strangely uncomfortable. "She could do better," he said.

"Yes, she could," Mrs. Chalmers said and squeezed his arm. "You might remember that, before you come to some rash decision. You might also remember that I did not live to be this old without cultivating good woman's instincts—you might even call me somewhat psychic. So do an old lady a favor, and stick around. You enjoy yourself and when the party's over, we'll talk. If you don't like what you hear, then that will be that."

Steve started to protest, but glanced at Molly and thought, *What will it hurt?*

"Okay," he said.

"Can I trust you to mingle?"

"But of course." Steve smiled at her. "But I do need to use the restroom first."

Mrs. Chalmers directed him through another room and down the hall. He found the bathroom, used it and then moved through the house away from the party room. Soon he found himself in the drawing room where he'd first met Mrs. Chalmers. How much she knew about how he felt about Molly bothered him a great deal. He prided himself on being stoic in front of clients about his personal feelings.

170

Of course, taking her granddaughter and the girls for pizza might have given her a clue, Einstein, he thought. Of course. Psychic, my butt.

Steve seated himself on the sofa in front of the fireplace and leaned forward and snagged the large coffee-table book in front of him. *Witches and the Occult* by Merrilee. No last name. "Catchy," Steve said out loud. He settled and opened the book. On the title page he found the book was signed, with today's date. "To Carlotta, best regards, Merrilee" it read. Steve began to thumb through it. It was selectively illustrated primarily with woodcuts and photos of ancient paintings depicting witches and the devil. He turned to the back of the book and checked the index for *Das Fayden*. Page 70. He flipped back and found the page. The ancient illustration was of a hag and a princess both holding a large book, each one trying to get it away from the other. The book was huge and had the same strange pentagram with another inside just like the medallion. Katzmer had been right—everyone thought the book was big, even way back in the 1700s when this depiction had been first cut in wood, dabbed in ink and pressed on parchment.

The copy under the picture was short and read: *"Das Fayden,* the book of the Convergence, believed to have the power to change the natural order of the Universe (see Virgin Child, p. 84)."

Steve began turning the pages one by one, his goal, page 84—when he realized that he was not alone. Her presence felt like a warm heat on the back of his neck. He stopped turning the pages. A hint of rich perfume wafted under his nose. It made him think of sex.

Steve stood up and pivoted, the book in his hands.

"Ah," said the woman in a black silken over-one-shoulder evening gown. Steve guessed her to be in her early forties. She was about five feet six. Her blond hair fell to her shoulders and framed her face like a helmet. Her brown eyes were large and seductive; and without really realizing it at first, he found himself staring at her ample cleavage. He looked up, embarrassed.

She smiled, walked around the sofa, and extended her hand as if he should kiss it. "Yes, yes," she said, in approval of him.

Steve took her hand. There was something very sexual about the feel of her grip. She had a slight smile on her face.

"Merrilee," she said.

"Steve Brogan," he said and raised the book. *The* Merrilee?"

"Yes. Why? Are you interested in the occult, Steve?"

Steve realized that he was still holding her hand and released it. She sat down on the sofa

172

and Steve sat down beside her and opened the book to page 70. "Not a lot. Just selectively. He stabbed at the picture with a finger. This book in particular. And everything about it. There's not much printed."

"That's because not much is known, and now you and I are into an area of research of my new book. Funny, isn't it how fate draws two people together?" She reached out and touched the photograph, letting her arm rest against his as she pointed to the pentagram on the book. She tapped it with her index finger.

She's flirting with me, thought Steve, and moved his hand away from her.

She looked up at him and smiled. "I'm from New York. I'm out here on a research trip for the new book. Carlotta Chalmers was kind enough to invite me tonight, and I really think it rude to be here talking when we should be at the party. Look, I'm staying at the Vanguard Hotel in Sherman Oaks. You know the new one that looks a mile high where the freeways cross. Do you know it?"

"Yes."

"Why don't you come by tomorrow at ten o'clock, and we'll do brunch. The hotel has an excellent restaurant. I'll answer all your questions, and we can get to know each other. I'm here for several weeks. It would be nice to have some intelligent conversation. I can go over my notes on *Das Fayden* with you—the Virgin

Child, The Convergence, everything. It will help me prepare for my work here . . ."

"Oh there you are," interrupted Thom in a flat, lifeless voice.

Merrilee turned around at the same time as Steve, and Steve couldn't tell who he was speaking to. His eyes shifted from Merrilee to Steve and back again.

"What can we do for you?" Merrilee asked with an icy tone of voice.

Maybe she doesn't like Thom, either, thought Steve.

Thom shifted his gaze back to Steve. "Mrs. Chalmers asked me to look for you. She requests that you rejoin the party."

"We'll be right there," said Merrilee imperiously. She meant, leave us alone, but Thom didn't budge.

Steve stood up and held out his hand. Merrilee took it, and stood up. They followed Thom back to the party area, and over to Mrs. Chalmers and Molly.

"I was afraid you had gotten lost," said Mrs. Chalmers.

"So was I," Molly said to Steve, giving Merrilee a sidelong glance. She looked disturbed, jealous maybe, Steve thought. Oh, he wished.

Thom continued to stare at him angrily.

The piano began playing a nice melody. And though no one else was dancing, Merrilee took Steve's hand and pulled him into a dance position. Instinctively his arms came up, and he looked around, embarrassed. "I'm not much of a dancer, Merrilee."

She didn't seem to care because she started moving and Steve had to follow along. She was light and felt great in his arms. She looked at Thom and said, "He's such a nice man, don't you think, Mr. Lusk?"

And Steve saw Thom murder him with his eyes.

They danced a small distance away.

"Thom has got an attitude," offered Steve.

"He is annoying, isn't he?"

"Oh, yeah. That he is."

They danced for a moment, passing by people standing, and smiling as they moved by. Finally another couple joined the floor. Steve felt relieved, but he could tell Merrilee didn't care what anybody thought. She just did what she felt like. And in a way, Steve envied her that abandon.

"You think I'm too forward, don't you, Steve?"

"I think people should just be who they are," he said and for some reason this must have struck Merrilee as being very funny, because she laughed a shrieking laugh, the likes of which neither Steve nor anyone else had ever heard.

The pianist changed to an up-tempo beat, and Merrilee danced faster, but never let go of Steve.

And the night wore on.

The party thinned gradually, and Steve was surprised that it ended so soon. By ten o'clock Thom had made his excuses and left. Merrilee left at ten-thirty, but only after extracting a promise that Steve would come to brunch (which Molly overheard and it pleased Steve that the invitation seemed to frost her). By midnight he was alone in the party room with Mrs. Chalmers, Molly, the dwarf sisters, Radella and Radinka, Motu, and the two big dogs.

Steve was seated in a winged-back chair in the corner. And all but Motu were seated on two sofas near Steve. Motu knelt down with the two dogs near the fireplace.

Steve spoke first. "Look, I've become attached to you all. I believe you to be good people, but I am responsible for others and I have to make decisions with them in mind." He reached into his coat pocket and pulled out the paper with the copy of the design found on the medallion drawn on it. "I found a medallion with this stamped on it when I went to the grave site. Following up on this I contacted a man who is an expert in the occult and he gave me the number of Lady May, Queen Witch of the Coven of the Crystal Moon, and that turns out to be you, Mrs. Chalmers. And I think I've gone far enough with my investigation.

"Present company excepted, my opinion of people who dabble in occult matters is not very high, I'm afraid. So, I'm going to terminate my involvement as of now. And suggest to you that you leave it up to the police."

Molly's eyes widened, then narrowed. "You've got a date with Merrilee tomorrow to discuss this, I was told."

"I'll cancel it, Molly," he said.

No one spoke for a few moments; they seemed like an eternity to Steve. Steve was about to stand and leave when Carlotta rose herself and said, "In the fifteenth century Universal Powers were discovered and their access written down in a book, *Das Fayden,*" she said. "The book was hidden or lost, and no one knows where, but from its teachings two Covens sprang forth: The Coven of the Crystal Moon and the Coven of the Dark Dream. Throughout history these two Covens have been at odds, but in the last seventy years, there has been no hostility, and it has appeared that the Coven had disappeared.

"We had thought that, up until recently with desecration of my sister's grave."

"Why is that?" Steve asked, focused on her every word.

"Because my sister and I had a falling-out for some years and she went her way and I continued with my way. It was only when she died that I learned that she had dedicated her life to the Devil. She had sought out the remnants of the Coven of the Dark Dream and sold her soul and revitalized their evil."

"But she's dead, now."

"Yes, I know. Her body was returned to us, found cut in six pieces in a small hotel outside of Bakersfield: extremities and head removed— it's the mark of the devil, Mr. Brogan. Through some investigation we were able to determine that my sister, Mary J. Hull, had obtained the stature of Queen of the Coven of the Dark Dream. She was known as The Great Jobina, Queen of the Coven of the Dark Dream. Her following was small and all but died out with her passing.

"And you see before you members of the Coven of the Crystal Moon . . ."

"All of you?" Steve looked at Molly.

"Yes, all of us," Molly said. "And there's more that you are going to have difficulty with, but I want you to listen to Lady May. She is our Queen, she is my grandmother, and she too is a Great Lady, just like Jobina, except for the powers of good."

Steve sat back in his chair and shifted his gaze to Mrs. Chalmers, who continued with her story: "The time has come for a great happening. It is foretold. It involves the *Das Fayden,* the planetary alignments, the hands of glory, and the Virgin Child.

"All that we have right now is the Virgin Child. You see throughout the centuries the Queen of the Coven of the Crystal Moon was the Virgin Child, before her ascension to status of Queen."

"Virgin Child, like Mary and Jesus."

"Somewhat. Each of us gave birth to our first child without benefit of intercourse. That is the way, and was the way until Molly broke with tradition and had intercourse with a man before the birth of her Virgin Child Offspring. So, it stops with her. She is the last Virgin Child, the sign of the coming of the Convergence. Within our beliefs, our rituals, the Convergence has been verified as being at hand, and now with the assault on the grave of my sister, the stealing of her hands, it appears that the Coven of the Dark Dream is alive and well.

"But still, there was not enough proof, until recently, when a member of their Coven contacted us. A high member who was disgraced. Her name is Anna Kleiber, and I wish you to speak with her. She's in hiding. What she has to tell you, will chill your heart, Steve."

Mrs. Chalmers held her hands out to her sides indicating everyone present. Our existence is threatened, and we need your help. Somewhere, *Das Fayden* may have surfaced . . ."

"It has," said Steve. "The expert I saw today has it."

"It's a large book, with hinges," said Mrs. Chalmers, with thinly veiled guile in her voice.

"It's a small book, the size of a paperback . . ."

"Ah! You have seen it!"

The group murmured.

"It has been foretold," said Radinka.

"Foretold," mimicked Radella.

Molly stood up and moved very close to Steve. He thought her truly beautiful in her green sparkling evening gown. "We believe that we are under attack, by the Dark Coven. And we need your expertise to protect us, Steve."

"Why don't you hex them, or whatever it is that witches do, and protect yourselves, Molly? You're witches, aren't you?" He felt a lump in his throat as he said it. It was rude and meant to distance him from her.

She didn't take the bait. She said in a matter-of-fact tone, "With the Convergence we must conserve our power. We can little afford to spare any at all . . ."

Steve stood up, towering over Molly. He said, "I don't want to be a part of this. I don't believe in witches and goblins and magic. In fact, before I met you, I had a very negative image of anyone who gets mixed up in this kind of stuff. But I have responsibilities . . ."

"We are your responsibilities, too, Steve. You agreed to help us."

"I don't believe in this hocus-pocus stuff, and if the other group of people who are after you get out of line then call the police."

"Who would believe us, Steve?"

"Not many, that's for sure."

Molly searched his face. "You're not a coward," she stated. "But you're afraid."

180

"What I'm afraid of is that I'm losing my judgment . . . I thought you were a little more level."

Anger flashed across Molly's face, and Steve felt an angry heat from her. "Everything y'know is nothing compared to the Knowledge," she said. "You want proof, is that what you want?"

Steve shrugged, feeling he had already lost Molly. "Okay. If you give me proof, then I'll help you. Then I'll risk my people."

Molly looked down for a moment then looked up at him. "Today you might have had a dream or an urge about Daphne . . ."

Steve stared at her.

"You did," said Molly. She must have seen it in his eyes.

"So what," said Steve.

"She was playing with my spell book today and because she likes you she cast a romantic spell on you. I caught it before it could go any further."

"I said *proof*," Steve said. "That's too coincidental. I was thinking of asking you and the girls to go for pizza earlier today, it would be normal for me to think of one of you."

Steve stood up and looked around the room. "If that will be all, I'll be going, now." He glanced at Molly. "I'm sorry it didn't work out."

"Daphne told me that if I asked you, you would help me. She has never been wrong."

Steve said nothing for a moment. Everyone

else was silent. He searched the faces of the people, and then the blue-eyed dogs.

"Make me a believer," he said, "and I will help you."

No one said a word. "I thought so." He turned and walked toward the threshold of the party room.

"I suppose you'll be sending me a bill," said Mrs. Chalmers.

Steve turned around to answer, and gasped. Everyone in the room, including the dogs, was floating in midair, four feet off the ground.

Fifteen

WINGED THINGS

Katzmer reached out and turned on another lamp, and pulled it on its spring-tension arm and drew it closer to the medallion. He picked up a pair of rubber-tipped tweezers and moved the magnifying stand over the coin then picked it up gently with the tweezers and leaned further over to examine the writing.

But wait. He heard something. He did not jerk his head up. He listened. After so many years in this old attic of the cathedral, he knew every creak and moan of the old girl's timbers and stones. Even the tap-tap pecking of the pigeons against the stained-glass had become mundane to him, a sound filed away and never really heard.

But this, rapping, not tapping, was secretive and purposeful. And that scared Katzmer. Because all of that was happening some hundred feet off the ground; and what manner of creature could do that?

There! Finally he heard the breaking of a pane of glass. It was down the east corridor.

A sinking feeling pressed him to his seat, but he knew that he had to do something. He heard more glass breaking, and thought how stupid he'd been not to light the attic better. The switches for what lights he did have were way down the south corridor by the entrance. He had lighting in his immediate area, but down the east corridor it was dark, and spooky looking.

He put down the medallion and set the tweezers down beside it. He bolted suddenly from his chair into the west wing darkness where knights' armor stood on their stands, leaving the medallion and *Das Fayden* on the table. He pulled a poleax from one set of armor and backed into the darkness behind a display case.

An eerie silence followed, so long that Katzmer was beginning to feel foolish. Maybe some old display case had cracked or crashed under the weight of some antique armor piled on top. Maybe it hadn't been a pane of glass that had broken. And why had he left the medallion and *Das Fayden* behind like that? Scaredy-cat.

Katzmer had just decided to head back to the table, when the closest arched stained-glassed window in the east wing exploded inward, and something tumbled to the ground. The noise was deafening, and Katzmer cringed at the sound. His heart trip-hammered in his chest at what he saw shaking itself off, stretching its huge grey wings to remove shards of glass. Even in the weak light cast from Katzmer's workstation he could make out much of the thing's detail. It stood seven feet tall and was roughly the shape of a very thin naked man. Two tennis-ball sized eyes bulged from the thing's thin face. Its mouth was partially open, its lips pulled permanently back, revealing long ragged, razor-sharp teeth. It leaned forward from the waist, tucked its wings on its back and hobbled toward the lit workstation, with its sinewy arms extended in front of him.

Katzmer moved back further behind the display.

Suddenly there was another noise. A small tinkling of glass this time.

Katzmer glanced quickly up at the broken window and saw another thing. It hopped out of the broken window, stretched its wings and glided down to the floor. It was basically the same as the other winged-thing except it was larger, and it carried a passenger.

A man detached himself from the second flying thing's back. He was wearing blue jeans, a heavy leather coat, and an old-style World War I leather flying helmet, with goggles and a scarf wrapped around his neck. He pulled off the leather gloves and walked toward the other creature and into the light. The man scanned the lit area.

He's looking for something, thought Katzmer,

his heart still racing in his chest. His mouth felt dry and adrenaline made his hands shake.

The man stepped up to Katzmer's work desk. He reached out and picked up *Das Fayden* and then the coin. "Here," he said with appropriate awe in his voice. He knew what he was after.

Katzmer felt a sickness of fear and anger consume him like a fire. He wanted to charge forward, but his legs wouldn't. He couldn't even pull himself back to safety. He was frozen.

He watched the man flip through the book. He raised it high and said, "Blessed is the Book—Blessed is *Das Fayden.*" He lowered his hands and tucked the book and medallion in his coat. He pulled his gloves from inside the coat and put them on. Then he turned to mount his creature.

And Katzmer charged.

What had broken him free he wasn't sure, but as he ran forward, he screamed and was thinking about the book. He had to get that book.

The nearest creature spun around just as Katzmer sliced at him with the poleax, cutting a slice of wing membrane. The creature howled and swatted at him with a huge claw, and hopped around to fully face him.

"Radd," the man called out. "Kill him quickly, we have no time."

The wounded creature sprang at him. Katzmer sidestepped and poked with the poleax. The creature sidestepped too, and escaped the blow. It grabbed the shaft behind its head. It pulled

186

hard with its powerful arm and yanked Katzmer up off his feet into a sprawl on the floor.

Katzmer scrambled backward and to his feet.

The thing leered at him, and bared its teeth: they were long yellow fangs. Its eyes were the eyes of savage death.

Katzmer ran.

The thing sprang at the same time Katzmer dove behind a display case. He had one chance and on instinct alone he was up and headed for it—a workman's nook, one of eight that had been necessary to build the cathedral's arched roof.

The display case crashed behind. Katzmer heard a flutter of wings and growl and a swipe across his back. Its blow grazed him and propelled him forward, knocking the wind out of Katzmer. Gasping for breath he scrambled toward a pillar and ducked behind just as the thing hit full force on the wall.

Katzmer inhaled a deep breath and backed up behind the pillar.

The thing turned and grabbed, but Katzmer had found the workman's niche and backed into it. The creature was too large to squeeze in, but he could reach, and that he did, barely missing Katzmer's face with a rake of foul smelling talons.

Katzmer pressed further back and down and he knew the thing couldn't get to him.

The man in the flying suit called, "Radd,

come! No one will believe him! We go! You can come back another time!"

The thing eyed Katzmer with almost-human disdain. It opened its mouth and said in a bass voice, "I'll be back for *you,* small thing."

It backed out from between the support pillar and the wall and Katzmer heard it *clop-clop* away, and soon heard the flapping of its wings as it lifted off the floor and out the window where it had broken in.

Steve was staring at Carlotta Chalmers floating four feet off the ground when his phone rang. He reached inside his pocket and pulled it out. Mrs. Chalmers had let the others down gently and was staying aloft until Steve verified that she was not wearing wires.

He waved her down. He was convinced. And she floated gently down with a satisfied smile on her face.

Molly said, "I hope you're happy, Steve. We need all her power, and it takes a lot to do that. You *will* help us, now, won't you?"

"I'd be breaking my word if I didn't," he said, a feeling of dark premonition about the phone call overcoming him.

He flipped open the phone and took the call.

It was his service, and they gave him the message that Katzmer had called and that it was an emergency. Steve took the number, gave an apologetic look at the group, and made the call.

The phone was answered right away and it was Katzmer. "Steve," he said like he'd known Steve all his life, "you've got to come to the museum. You've got to come. You won't believe until you see."

"See what?"

"Just come, please. And bring a gun."

"Call the police."

"NO! NO POLICE!"

"Okay. Are you in danger, now?"

"I think I'm okay, for now. Just come."

"Tell me more. I'm coming, but tell me what's wrong."

"Winged things, Steve. I know it sounds crazy, but winged things. Monsters. They came and stole the *Das Fayden* and the medallion. And I got a piece of one of its wings. I got it to show you."

"I'll be right there," said Steve. "Just hang on. I'll be right there."

Steve folded his phone and put it back in his jacket. He addressed Mrs. Chalmers. "Do you know anything about 'winged things'? I've come across two people who have seen them, and I need to know what they are."

For the first time since he had met her, Mrs. Chalmers seemed truly disturbed. "Did they describe them?"

"Just monsters, my contact said."

Mrs. Chalmers exchanged worried looks with Molly, then said, "Since you are not a believer . . ."

"Pretend I'm a believer. I'm acting now on that assumption. It makes it easier for me."

Mrs. Chalmers took his measure for a second then explained, "The body is physical and ethereal. A trained person on the wrong side of the pentagram can suck that ethereal part out of the person, and mold it into anything that person wants. In legend the worst of these are Winged Things called Hadesmorphs, and they are traditionally the enforcers and guards of the Queen of the Coven of the Dark Dream. It takes a lot of baby essence to make the Hadesmorph . . ."

"Baby essence?"

"Yes. The Dark Coven is run on baby essence, it's extracted from babies' blood through ritual, and it is never wasted because it is precious . . . but this Dark Queen has found a terrible way to make sure she has plenty of the essence, but that is why you must meet the woman who escaped . . . she will tell you all . . . and you will believe."

"Okay," said Steve. "I've got to take care of the call right now. Where and when do you want to meet you and the person?"

"Tomorrow morning at ten-thirty at the Bon Adventure Hotel," said Molly. "Meet me in the lobby and I'll take you up."

"Okay," said Steve. It meant he would have to reschedule with Merrilee. He asked Molly to walk him to his car.

190

They said nothing to each other as they walked and when they reached his Cadillac, he asked her, "Do you know what *war footing* is?"

"No."

"It's a state of readiness in time of war or impending war. I want you and your Coven people to go on war footing from now on. This man I'm going to see, had possession of *Das Fayden* and those things stole it. In other words, things are heating up and you . . . your Coven people . . . need to be in a state of readiness . . ."

"Things are being prepared . . ."

"I know that you are *aware*. And that Carlotta is doing her magic spells and stuff. But that's not what I mean. You've got to think and act in every manner a hundred percent aware that something is moving against you."

Molly started to protest.

"No. I'm an expert in these matters. I'm telling you that right now your people don't have the proper attitude . . . start thinking defensively. Guards. This party should have never taken place—its too dangerous."

"Steve." (She reached out and touched his arm. He savored the feel of it). "By having a child before giving birth to the next Virgin Child, I ruined the cycle. Whatever the Dark Coven wants to do they need the Virgin Child and there is none . . ."

"Yes, but they don't know that."

"Good point."

"War footing," emphasized Steve. "Do you

have people in your Coven who can protect you?"

"Carlotta's magic and Motu and Cotu, his brother."

"If you're the Virgin Child, and they think they need you, you better get away. Go into hiding."

"Thom has asked me and the kids to go meet his family. I was putting him off."

Steve hesitated only a moment. "Does he know about this thing, about your religion?"

"A little, but he's not interested. He believes in freedom of religion and we just don't discuss the white witchcraft part of this."

Steve wanted to ask her what she saw in that stiff, but he knew she wanted to hide in his stability. There was nothing he could to do about it. "So he knows nothing about *Das Fayden?*"

"Nothing," she said and removed her hand.

Steve felt an emptiness consume him briefly but went on with what he knew was best. "Okay, you do this. After we meet tomorrow go with him. Will he leave tomorrow?"

"He's his own boss. He said we could go anytime."

"Okay, you leave tomorrow. And you stay gone; you should be safe. Make sure your grandmother knows where you're going and the phone number, but have her keep it to herself. You can give it to me tomorrow." Steve opened the car door and got in. He closed the door and rolled down the window. "I'm with you now,

Molly . . . this White Magic Coven thing is new to me, but I'm with you now. Do you understand?"

Molly looked at him in a contemplative manner for a few seconds, then she nodded in understanding. She knew that he had promised on his sacred honor to do everything he could to help her and her family.

"Thank you," she said.

He nodded, started his car, and drove off to meet Katzmer and hear more about winged things.

Steve stopped by the office briefly before going on to the museum. From his arms locker he pulled a Beretta nine-millimeter with two full extra clips, shoulder holster, and a riot shotgun, with twenty-five extra rounds of ammunition.

The car clock glowed 3:30 as Steve drove up the driveway of the museum.

Katzmer had said to bring a gun, and Steve was going to take him at his word, and enter armed for bear.

He parked near a '67 VW bus that he assumed was Katzmer's auto. All of the lights in the museum appeared to be on, and as he retrieved his shotgun from the trunk and loaded the tube magazine first with three double-ought buckshot shells, then two rifled-slugs shells, he spotted raw light streaming out of a broken stained-glass window on the top section of the cathedral.

Steve jacked a round into the chamber, slipped a rifled slug in the magazine to take its place, and started toward the door. It was closed, but unlocked, and Steve entered cautiously, closing the door quietly behind him. He padded through the antechamber and then to the stairs and up where he knew he would find Katzmer.

The attic was as he remembered it except it was lit with artificial lights that cast strange shadows on the wall. He strode quickly to Katzmer's desk. He pivoted on one foot until he had looked in all directions. Finally, he called out, "Katzmer! Katzmer!"

He heard a muffled reply. And then footsteps and finally Katzmer appeared with a pike in one hand and a short sword in the other. He shuffled quickly over to Steve. "You aren't going to believe this," he said, and Steve could see on his face the man was scared.

"Try me."

Katzmer recounted his story and when he was done he produced a bundle and opened it carefully. He lifted a ragged flap of grey membranous skin. Steve estimated it to be about ten inches long by six inches wide.

Katzmer's voice was shaky as he spoke, "And the thing told me he would come back for me. I didn't call the police. They wouldn't believe me, I'm sure."

Steve said, "Wrap it up and put it back in your pocket."

Katzmer did so, saying, "I've called a friend, he's going to meet me at his lab at six this morning. He's going to check it out, the cell structure, etc. I know that you're a skeptic but I'm telling the truth, I swear it."

"Okay," said Steve, finally relaxing a little and checking out the hole in the stained-glass window. He sat down on a stool and leaned the shotgun against a bench. "I'm a different man than you met yesterday. I need your help and apparently you need my help if this thing's telling you it'll be back. And I'm wondering if you want to join forces, so to speak?"

"Yes," Katzmer said without hesitation. "I was scared, but I finally charged the thing. Stupid me. But when I saw him stealing the *Das Fayden,* I couldn't stand it. I've got my reputation on the line and nothing but a photocopy to back it up."

"A photocopy?"

"Yeah, with all the handling I needed to do, it saves wear and tear to photograph the pages and use those for the majority of the work."

Steve said, "Okay, you get the copy and you get home and get some sleep . . . by the way, how do you think they knew that you had the *Das Fayden?*"

"My paper is being published next month, and somehow they found out. My editor may have said something—probably did, because this is big

195

news. I told him not to. Or a copy editor, or some other way. I really don't know."

Steve checked his watch. It was four-thirty in the morning. He needed to get home and get what rest he could for the day ahead. He walked around with Katzmer as Katzmer locked the museum. "I'm closing the museum for the time being," Katzmer said.

Steve gave him his card and his pocket telephone number and car phone number. "Call me when your friend finds out what this thing is," he said. "And I need to know if I can count on you if this situation turns hot."

"In the interest of knowledge, I will help you, but I want you to know that I'm not James Bond—I don't even like his movies."

Steve laughed, then said, "Remember that everything you do is to save your own ass, too. Until you kill that thing you're never gonna know any real peace of mind."

"I know," said Katzmer. "Now can we get out of here?"

Steve and Katzmer drove down the drive, VW bus following Steve's Cadillac at Katzmer's request. They pulled out on the street and stopped while Katzmer got out and closed and locked the gates. As Steve watched Katzmer fumble with the gate lock he thought that he liked this Katzmer. Pretty brave guy for a civilian, that was for sure.

Katzmer regained his bus, and pulled up beside and unrolled his window. "I want in on this, Steve. Don't leave me out, okay? It's my life's work that's jumped out of dusty old books and into reality. I want to know everything."

"Katz, don't worry about it. I need your expertise. Do you know how to use a gun?"

Katzmer smiled. "I was an Israeli commando in the Sinai. I can shoot. Little rusty, but it'll come back." He waved and drove off engulfed in the coughing rattling of his old VW engine.

Sixteen

MERRILEE

The penthouse of the luxurious Vanguard Hotel cost a fortune each day, but money at this point in her life was not a problem. It fitted her needs perfectly with the all-important roof access and large open balcony—and of course, total privacy.

She had alerted the management that Steve Brogan was her guest and he was to be allowed above the thirty-fifth floor. The hotel guard at that point would escort him to a private elevator and he could ascend to a beautiful mini-breakfast buffet, complete with champagne. A chef would arrive shortly, cook the omelets to order, and then disappear, leaving her alone with Steve Brogan, his questions, and hopefully his body. After that he would be hers, if he was any kind of man at all. And she had lots to do to him, that was for sure.

Last night he seemed immune to her charm

and that had infuriated her, though she was careful not to let it show. She should not have to beg. He should and would consider it a privilege to have slept with her, once he had succumbed.

The phone rang. That would be hotel service announcing Steve Brogan.

"Hello." She heard Steve Brogan's voice, and right away she knew it was bad news.

"Hello, Steve. Are you in the lobby?" she asked, knowing that he wasn't.

"No, I need to take a rain check."

"Why?"

"I can't explain, now. But, can I call you in a day or so and reschedule?"

"No. Give me your number. I will call you when I get back. I'm really mad at you. I've gone to a lot of trouble to have a nice brunch prepared. I even hired a chef. Cancel your other appointment. I promise to be a good interview."

She heard him sigh. "If I could, I would. I need to talk to you, but I truly have no choice."

He gave her his number, apologized again and hung up.

She stood up and screeched, "Damn him!"

The double doors to the bedroom opened, and Sloat rushed out. Cutter and Radd followed in their deceptively slow hobble. They had done well the night before and she had praised them, so they were content.

"What is it, Mother?" Sloat asked.

She pulled out the pins that held on her blond helmet of a wig, then pulled the wig off and flung it across the room. "Nothing!" She pulled out the pins that held her hair up and shook out her river of fine black hair that fell down to her ankles. "I'll take the contacts out later."

Sloat said, "Do you want me to kill him?"

Cutter and Radd giggled with anticipation at the question.

"No. No. He is not to be killed. I can turn him. I just need some time." Every once and a while there came a person whose mind she could not violate—she got no impressions from him other than those of the five senses, and it bothered her. If she were at the Caverns, it might be different. She had more power there.

"What do you see in him?" The question was ripe with jealousy. She had warned him against that, but he had done well in the night and had brought her *Das Fayden,* and the location of the traitor Anna Kleiber, so she did not scream at him.

"The girl he sent to spy on us told me much. She was correct, he is a handsome man, and I want him, Sloat." Her face became as a scowling mask as she spoke. "Once he knows his spy is missing he will come for her. Or, send someone for her . . . I can't take that risk. I want him under my control, now."

"What is so important about him, Mother?" said Sloat. "He is nothing. Let me kill him."

She spun around and confronted Sloat now, the full power of being Lady Eva, Queen of the Coven of the Dark Dream, radiating from her like fiery death. She pointed a long, thin finger at him. "I forbid harm to him! And if anything happens to him, I will hold you responsible! I have plans for the protector of their Coven! Now, leave me!" She raised her hand imperiously in dismissal.

They obeyed her.

And good riddance, she thought. She had work to do now. The Convergence was at hand. She had the book, now they needed the Virgin Child. The Medallions would come back on their own—this had been foretold. But, now she had to rid the Universe of Anna Kleiber the traitor. She had not allowed Sloat to kill her last night, because her escape was a very personal matter and angered her beyond belief. Lady Eva relished the dark tangy pleasure of revenge.

She stripped naked, picked her anthame, her sharp witch's knife, and a small vial of baby essence, then walked out on the totally private section of the penthouse patio. At thirty-six stories, she had privacy from casual passers-by. And the line of sight from above was restricted by an awning and privacy fencing on the patio.

She brought her forearm to her face and sprinkled baby essence on it, dropped the bottle and slit deep into her forearm with the anthame, then pulled it out and let her blood flow to the flooring below. She urinated where she stood, relishing the warmth of the fluid down her leg. Finally she knelt and snagged the dropped bottle and emptied the rest of its contents on top of her own spilled blood. She then spit in it and held her arm over it to mix more blood, drop by drop.

The wound had been deep, but now, and because she was the Queen of the Dark Dream, it was fast healing. She must finish casting the spell before the wound healed completely. She mixed the fluids quickly on the cement surface with her fingers, then used the fluid mix to draw the sacred and unholy inverted pentagram.

She began to chant as she traced over the pentagram time and time again, and finally she felt the vile fire within her and she said the words, and knew her word would be done.

Seventeen

ANNA KLEIBER

Steve walked over to the window and looked out over Los Angeles. From twenty-three floors up he could see a lot: the morning crawl on the freeways, the traffic down below; the City Hall's tower and the surrounding skyscrapers in the distance.

Molly was inside the bathroom helping Anna Kleiber, the escapee from the Dark Coven, clean up.

Steve caught sight of a commercial airliner in the distance descending from the blue sky into the smoggy mess that was the atmosphere in Los Angeles. He wondered about those people and how they would feel if they were told that something really major was about to happen, that would affect them, and that thing was supernatural in nature. Steve snorted. They would laugh at him. He must always remember that no one would believe him, or that it would take too much time to prove what he was saying was true. Hell, less than a week ago, he would have been one of those people.

Not now. Not after what Anna Kleiber had disclosed. Because he believed her, and he always trusted his instincts in that department. She had told him everything, including the baby factory, the layout of the Caverns. He had asked her about ventilation and power and the like, and though not knowing a lot of the detail, she did know that once the Caverns had been found by the Great Jobina, that engineers from the Coven had been brought in and had arranged power, water, and gas.

Of everything she talked about, the story of Sloat and how he was sacrificed and supposedly brought back to life disturbed him the most. If he assumed that the winged things, the Hadesmorphs existed, then what the hell, maybe this Sloat could exist.

He put his head in hands and closed his eyes for a moment. He didn't usually think like this. It turns reality upside down, and it was hard to take on many levels.

The bathroom door opened and Molly wheeled out Anna Kleiber, who smiled weakly. The door connecting this suite to another opened and Cotu, whom Steve had met only minutes before, stuck his head in. He was Motu's brother and the woman's bodyguard and a half a head taller and thicker than Steve. "Just checking," he said and closed the door, leaving them to privacy. He had been with her since she had been picked up some days ago.

"Okay," said Steve. "What I need to know is about the Convergence. Tell me what you know."

"It is predicted to be very soon. Within days from now. Every member of the Coven of the Dark Dream will be there. Some have already arrived. The ritual will take place in the Cavern and it will install and empower Lady Eva as a literal Goddess of the Earth—a Dark Goddess for sure. She has made a pact with the devil and she is pure evil."

"What about the prerequisites for the ritual child, the *Das Fayden*, et cetera."

"They found them all. That's what my husband told me just before I escaped. All they needed to do was to collect them."

Steve stood up and moved over to the window and stared at the sky. It wasn't clear blue anymore, a small gathering of dark clouds had appeared. He examined them as he said, "But who is the Virgin Child? Did he tell you that?"

The cloud formation was definitely odd. It was moving before his eyes.

"No. I don't think Lady Eva shared that with him."

"Come look at this, Molly." She stepped over and said, "Those look odd."

"Look, it's forming a symbol."

Anna Kleiber wheeled herself over and looked out. She screamed and started wheeling back quickly.

Steve looked at her and then back at the pentagram drawn in the tight, ugly black clouds.

Suddenly, lightning flashed, crashed through the window and hit Anna Kleiber. The bolt hit her in the stomach and ripped up her middle in a smoking blue light. The sickening smell of electrically charred flesh cloyed the room.

Another lightning bolt struck and fried Anna Kleiber's head. The stink of burning hair competed with the burned smell.

Cotu burst through the connecting door, but Steve grabbed Molly and pushed back against Cotu, shouting, "Get out! Get out! Let's get out of here!"

Steve shut the door behind them, and said, "Listen. In a minute there is going to be a bunch of people up here and the police. We'll have a lot of explaining to do and it will take days, believe me, and we just don't have the time. Remember war footing? Well if there is any doubt now, you're crazy. Let's get out of here, now."

Molly looked at the interconnecting door and started to protest.

"No," said Steve, dragging her towards the door. "There is no time, and you don't want to see what's left of her." Cotu grabbed a black bag he had and followed them out.

At this time of day most of the guests weren't in their rooms, but a few came out into the hall, and Steve walked normally by them. No good being seen running from the scene. At the elevators the doors opened and three hotel personnel got off and hurried down the hall.

Steve, Molly, and Cotu got in and rode it down, and made their way to the parking structure. Motu was waiting with a limousine.

Emergency vehicle sirens wailed in the distance.

Steve guided Molly about twenty feet away, out of earshot of Cotu. She looked in shock. And he shook her gently. "It'll probably get uglier from now on. I want you to get the girls and go find Thom and go visit his family. Call my office when you get there and talk only to me. I'll get the number and address from you. And stay out of sight. Tell Thom only as much as you have to. Do you understand?"

Molly shook her head. Her eyes searched his face. "What are you going to do?"

"I'm gonna take care of this, somehow. I can't explain now, but you need to get to safety, you and the girls. So get Thom and make him take you to meet his family now. I'll find these people of the Dark Dream and take care of it."

"What about the police?"

"Remember always that authorities take a lot of time and proof to be convinced, and we don't have much of either right now."

He took her back to Motu, and opened the door for her, and said, "Molly. I said go visit Thom but do me a favor and don't marry the guy without talking to me first."

Molly gazed into his face and opened her

mouth to ask why, but then nodded in understanding. "Okay, Steve. I'll tell Daphne and Penny hello for you."

Steve searched her face with his eyes. "Thanks, Molly."

"No," said Molly. "Thank you."

Molly got in and Steve closed the door. "Take care of them, Cotu," he said and Cotu gave him a thumbs up.

Steve walked to his car, got in and started it up. He had somewhere special to go. Somewhere that his instinct told him to go. It was one of those loose ends that sometimes dangled in his mind until he tied it up.

The one time he didn't pay attention and tie up that string was the Balatta Sting, and a lot of his people had died because of it.

Eighteen

CHADWICK

Under pretense of being an old shipmate, Steve found himself sitting in John Chadwick's private office, the door closed, and Chadwick just gaining his high-back executive chair behind his desk.

He had gone to seed, a balding man in his forties with a pot belly, and zealot's eyes. Steve made a mental note to tell Molly that she hadn't missed out on much.

"I'm embarrassed to say, Steve," began Chadwick, "but I don't remember you, but then how could you expect that, right? I mean with a couple of thousand guys on the old flattop."

Steve stopped looking at the Bible on Chadwick's desk, and decided he would just have to go for it, license be damned. He said, "I'm a little embarrassed myself, John, because I'm not from any reunion committee. I'm here to ask you a few questions about Molly Daniels. You probably know her as Molly Chalmers."

Chadwick stood up. "Get out of here, right now. Before I call the police and have you arrested."

Steve remained relaxed and eyed the man coolly. "Sit down, John," he said in a calm voice. "Molly Daniels is in danger and this information is important, and I am willing to break the law to get it. So sit down before I make you sit down."

John Chadwick stared at him for a moment, and then at the phone.

"Don't try it," said Steve, again in a calm reasonable voice. "I am an expert at making people suffer."

John Chadwick sat down.

Steve stood up and walked over and locked the door.

"If the phone rings," said Steve, "tell them you'll call them back."

Chadwick nodded. His face drained of blood in front of Steve's eyes. Now, his face was the color of milk.

Steve sat back down. "Okay. Tell me about Molly, the pregnancy, and why you didn't marry her."

Chadwick began to shake. "Just what I told the other guy. Why doesn't she leave me alone?"

"What other guy?" Steve asked quickly.

"Last night. The other guy she sent. I was at the market and going to my car, when this seedy guy pulls up in a van. He forces me into the van and he doesn't rob me, he asks about Molly."

"All right," said Steve his mind racing. "Whoever that was it was the bad guy. I'm the good guy. You'll just have to trust me on that. What did he look like?"

"Beady eyes, a long nose."

"Any distinguishing marks."

"No." Chadwick thought a moment. "Jewelry. I saw jewelry. Zodiac jewelry."

Steve fished in his pocket for his copy of the design on the medallion. "Did any of it look like this."

Chadwick sat up in his chair. "Yes. It was the largest piece."

Steve sat forward in his chair. He didn't like doing this, but the thought of anything happening to Molly and her family sickened him. He spoke calmly again to Chadwick, and said, "I will know if you are lying, so tell me exactly what you told this guy who accosted you."

Chadwick said, "He told me that if I told anyone his questions he would see me dead."

"I will take care of him for you. You don't have to be afraid—except of me, if I don't get the truth."

Chadwick cleared his throat and said, "I told him that I could not possibly be the Father of the girl because I'd had a vasectomy two years before I met Molly. She cheated on me . . ."

And Steve did not really hear the rest. He

stood up and raised a hand to stop him. "That's all I need to know. I believe you, and don't worry about the sleazy guy. I'll find him and I'll take care of him for you.

"And this conversation never took place. Understand?"

Chadwick nodded his head repeatedly.

Steve grimaced and left him to his business.

In his car, he made a phone call to the Chalmers residence. Motu answered and told Steve that Molly had already left. Steve told him, "Good. If she calls for some reason, tell her to call back at your number in an hour. That's how long it should take me to get there."

"Okay," said Motu.

Steve hung up and pulled out into traffic. And it was jammed. He hoped the freeway wasn't this bad, but when he got there it was.

It took him two hours to get to the Chalmers estate and even as he pulled in he knew something was dreadfully wrong.

Nineteen

MASSACRE

Carlotta Chalmers looked up from her writing desk and listened. Silence. The kids. They had gone with Molly to visit Thom's folks. Even up here in the upstairs study, she could always hear their laughter and squeals coming from somewhere, either inside or outside. The house without them was too, too quiet for Carlotta's liking.

She had already completed her morning ritual of protection. The most recent events had made her aware of how inadequately protected they were, so she decided to increase the frequency of the ritual. Today she would perform it seven times. It was almost time to undress and draw down the white power of healing and protection.

"Lady May?"

Carlotta turned around and saw Merrilee standing in the doorway.

"What a pleasant surprise," she said, a little shocked that she had gotten this far without

Motu or the dogs stopping her. And then, in a moment of prescience, it was clear to her. Motu and the dogs were dead, and Merrilee was to be feared, because Carlotta should have had all kinds of warning about Merrilee. But Merrilee had been able to come in right under her nose, and she hadn't a clue.

With a sinking feeling, she realized that what Steve had told Molly had been right, they had needed to be on a war footing.

"Your magic is weak, Lady May," said Merrilee. She smiled sweetly.

"Have you killed everyone, Lady . . . Eva, isn't it?"

Lady Eva floated into the room, three feet off the floor. That's how she had gotten up the stairs without Merrilee hearing her. The woman landed softly on the floor, not five feet from her.

"They're all dead. And now it's your turn to die."

Carlotta felt the rage bubble up inside her. "Do you think it is going to be that easy, you evil thing? Do you?"

"No," said Lady May. "It was not easy killing the Great Jobina, and as her sister, I'm sure it will not be easy killing you, witch. But, in the end, I will drink my fill of your blood, and bathe in your essence." She pointed a finger at her. "Challenge?"

Carlotta stood up, her gaze locking with that of Lady Eva's, as they both began to undress.

"Challenge," she said, formally accepting Lady Eva's proposal.

It would be a witch's duel, and it would be to the death.

Steve pulled up the drive of the Chalmers house, and was looking forward to briefing Mrs. Chalmers and maybe showboating a bit that he had been right to send Molly and the girls away. He also wanted to talk to her a bit about her dislike of Thom, and maybe gain insight about a course of action, once this shit was taken care of.

He really didn't know how important it was that Molly was not the Virgin Child. It made Daphne the Virgin Child, and the Coven of the Dark Dream knew that, now. But how had they found out about John Chadwick and his relationship to Molly?

Steve threw the lever in park and got out of the car. This was the first time Motu hadn't been there to greet him. Steve noticed that the front doors were wide open. He stepped quickly inside, and smelled the tangy cupric smell of fresh blood.

He strode into the hallway and stopped at the bottom of the stairs. Stuck on the newel posts at the bottom of the stairs were the heads of the two great danes, their blue eyes milked over. Hanging upside down from the landing, by thistle rope, like carcasses in a meat market, were the naked, eviscerated bodies of Motu, Radella and Radinka, and Carlotta Chalmers. Next to them the headless bodies of the dogs also hung.

On the wall opposite the bodies, painted in blood, was the inverted pentagram of the Coven of the Dark Dream.

For an instant, Steve forgot that Molly and the girls were with Thom, and he started up the stairs to find them. Then he stopped. They were safe. They were okay. Now, all he had to do was wait for her to contact him, and then he could make arrangements with her to go into deep hiding, while he sorted this out.

He turned and started to run out of the house, then turned back to the hanging corpses. "God bless your souls," he said. "I will avenge you, if I can. I swear it."

He no idea why he'd said that out loud, except maybe that he felt any act so heinously evil had to be railed against to show that it was not allowed.

Feeling guilty, because once again he was not going to call the police, he ran to his car, got in and headed for the office to make plans and wait for Molly's call.

Twenty

THOM

Night had overtaken them about half an hour ago, Molly estimated. The girls were tired from the long trip and a stop at McDonald's for dinner. They were asleep on the back seat of the big Cadillac.

Molly looked out into the night. Thom had left the main highway even before it got dark, and Molly thought about how black the night was out in the country.

"What does your father do, again, Thom?" she said. She felt a little numbed for some reason, a headache coming on.

"He's an international power broker," Thom answered, the light from the instrument panel casting a yellow tinge on his pale skin. He did not smile.

"Was it hard being raised by him?"

"No. Not really. Mother's strong enough to stand up to him, so, even though he wasn't always around, when he was, she was there to make sure I got good treatment."

Molly felt she was breaking new ground. Thom was typically close-mouthed about his youth. He had hinted at a terrible childhood on several occasions, and she had decided to let him tell her about it in his own time.

"Do think your parents will like us?"

"My dad loves little girls. It was little boys he was strict on. He's going to love you guys to death, believe me. And Mom loves children. They're looking forward to meeting you very much."

"Good. I'm still nervous, though. I know how you must have felt coming over to meet my family."

Thom ignored her lead into a conversation, so she sat back and watched the darkness. "It sure is nice and quiet out here," she tried again.

Thom said. "My parents have owned this cabin for a long time."

"What cabin?"

"We're going up that hill to a mountain cabin where you'll have a great time. The family is already there. It's a lodge actually. My dad owns it."

"I hope you didn't go to any trouble on my account."

"It wasn't any trouble," he said, slowing down and making a left on a small road. "They insisted."

Molly leaned forward and looked up at the

dark mountain ahead. "I need to call Carlotta when we get up to the cabin."

"They have a phone," said Thom. "I'd let you use the car phone but it doesn't work out here in the country."

"It's okay. I can wait." Molly had almost said Steve, instead of Carlotta. She felt guilty, now. She glanced quickly at Thom, like he might be reading her thoughts. The truth was that ever since Steve had taken them to the pizza parlor, she had spent a little part of each day thinking fondly of him. And he liked her, didn't he? Isn't that what he had meant about not getting married without talking to him? Sure it was.

But duplicity was something she abhorred. And wasn't this duplicitous, going to meet Thom's family, using them to hide from danger when in reality she might not even want the "safe" way of life Thom represented. He was quiet and sincere, and frankly sometimes a bore. And she wasn't sure she wanted to settle for that.

Should she tell him now. No, she decided. Later, after things had died down.

"We're almost there," said Thom. "Thirty minutes up the mountainside." He punched the accelerator and at the same time beat on the steering wheel. "Yessir, thirty minutes and we'll be there."

A bar of light etched from the rearview mirror reflected across Thom's ice-blue eyes, making a mark across his face that made him look like he was wearing a bandit mask.

"Someone's behind us," she said.

"It's okay," said Thom. "That's family."

The car was now tilted up at a steep angle as they powered up the hill.

"How can you be sure?"

"Look back."

Molly twisted around.

"I'm going to cut my lights twice," said Thom. "He'll blink once, pause and blink twice. Okay, I'm cutting my lights twice."

The car behind them blinked its headlights once, paused a moment then blinked twice.

"See. Told you."

Molly felt a twisting feeling in her gut. Another set of headlights appeared behind the first set. Then the car with the first set of headlights whizzed past them and took up a position ahead. It was a jeep, with armed men riding inside.

"Thom. What's going on?" she asked.

"Look out to the side," he said.

Her side of the road had a three-foot shoulder, then dropped into a black abyss. Then she saw it. Something huge, flying next to the car.

"They like it when we get close to home," said Thom.

"Hadesmorphs?" she said, fear filling her like water into a jug. Two of them, now.

"Yes," said Thom. "The one closest to you is Cutter; the other one is Radd. They've been with the Coven since the days of the Great Jobina."

Molly stifled a scream. She had the children to think of, and now was no time to lose control. "You know then that I'm not the Virgin Child, so Daphne can't be either. I told you about John Chadwick, and . . . y'know, Daphne is not, either. She is of mortal blood."

Thom laughed a horrid laugh. He looked at her with cold, dead eyes, and it made her feel dirty. "I sent Floyd Carlson to talk with Johnny Boy, and he spilled his guts."

"So then you know I'm speaking the truth."

"No," said Thom. "That pious prick thought you had screwed around on him. You see, he had a vasectomy a few years before that he hadn't gotten around to telling you about."

The impact of what he was saying hit her like a blow to the gut. "Daphne," she whispered incredulously.

"Yes. So you see, Molly my sweet sow, we have the Virgin Child, *Dus Fayden,* the hands of glory, the whole nine yards, and in a couple of nights the heavens will be aligned for the Convergence and Mommy Dearest, Lady Eva, will ascend into the ranks of the truly great. Greater than Lady Jobina ever dreamed of being. And the world will see a new age; a dark, dark age. And it will please my father greatly."

Molly fought panic. She couldn't jump out, she had the kids to think of. Her grandmother would come to help her, and Steve. Dear Steve.

And as if he knew what she was thinking, Thom said, "Oh, by the way, your granny is dead. So are the big ape and those twin midgets—the dogs, too, all dead."

Molly took the news like she had been physically hit. She convulsed in the seat, and then shuttered so much her teeth rattled. Carlotta dead. All of them, dead. The emotional pain became almost unbearable. He hadn't mentioned Steve. Good. He would come for them. He would avenge them.

"And the detective you hired. My mother has plans for him, in time. She fancies him, just like you do. But when she finishes with you, he won't have you. No man will have you." He laughed again his horrid laugh, and grinned at her.

My real name is Sloat, by the way. In the Coven of the Dark Dream I am the Lord High Executioner.

"Now, take your clothes off. I want to touch you all over. And if you don't give me any trouble, I won't kill Penny-Peanut, okay?" His grin twisted into a grimace, and then he laughed that ugly laugh again.

"Mommy?" Daphne asked sleepily. "What's going on? Why are you taking your sweater off?"

Molly turned to Daphne, thankful that Penny still slept. "It's okay, honey. I want you to lie back down, face the back of the seat, and go to sleep. Promise Mommy you'll do that, okay? Mommy needs you to do that, okay?"

For once Daphne didn't argue. She lay back

down with her face to the seat. She must have sensed the urgency of her mother's request.

"That's a good girl," said Molly.

Sloat reached out and put his right hand on her stomach, and for the first time she felt just how cold this Sloat was—as cold as a gravestone in the dead of a winter's night.

Twenty-one

POWWOW

Steve arrived at work and went immediately to his office. Soon, Ken Anderson stormed in and cornered him in his office. Steve was glad to see him. "Watching you is like watching the U.S. Cavalry ride in," said Steve.

Ken's eyes flared. "We've got problems—bigtime problems," he said. "You promised that if you got the crawl we would bail out. And you don't have to tell me you've got the crawl on this one, because I got it bad enough for both of us."

Steve pointed to the door. "Close it and sit down."

Ken did as he was told. And when he sat down, he was still bristling. "You just got in. Have you heard about Kay?"

"No."

"She's missed all her call-in times. I sent Montsano up to check on her, now he's missed his call-in times. I feel like taking the entire force up there and finding them, and wiping out any bad guys."

"Why didn't you tell me about Kay earlier?"

"Wasn't a problem earlier. She missed her call-in, but you and I both know that she's a free spirit like you and me and the time might not have been right. Now, what would you have done if she missed two call-ins in the initial part of the investigation?"

"Sent somebody to check it out."

"I sent Montsano to check it out. Now he's missed his call-in and I'm telling you about it."

Steve felt his gut cinch up and twist. Kay. Kay and all her enthusiasm. He wondered if he would end up writing a letter the way he had had to do too many times after the Balatta Sting. Montsano, too. Family man.

For a moment, he let himself dwell on this, and then he put it away. It didn't do anybody any good to tie himself up in knots. It was time now to act.

"Ken, I don't expect you to really believe what I'm about to tell you. I want you to listen. I want you to trust me that what I tell you has happened has really happened. And then I want you to call in as many of our A-team as you can find. Pull them off anything that they are on, and put them on this. Okay?"

Ken hesitated for more than a few seconds, taking Steve's measure, and coming to a decision. "We're in *deep-deep* shit, aren't we?"

"Up to our eyeballs."

Ken sighed. "Okay. Tell me what you got me into."

Steve spoke slowly and deliberately for five minutes straight, pausing only for emphasis, or to let a point sink in. Ken sat quietly the whole time, and when Steve was through, he folded his hands together over his stomach and eyed his hands as if they were of intense interest to him. Finally, he said, "If it were anyone but you, Steve, I'd tell them to get stuffed . . . but it *is* you. And I'm going to go with this thing, all the way to the end.

"What are we gonna do now?"

Steve had anticipated this, and in fact had been working on this on his drive back from the Chalmers massacre. "Tell Ira to make the calls to our guys to rendezvous here and have a pow-wow, and then go get our people."

"But the Caverns that Kleiber woman had talked about, did she tell you where they were?"

"She was paranoid and swapping information for care. She got fried before she told us."

Anderson stood up, and started pacing. "It's gonna make it tough."

"Maybe she told Molly. When she calls, I'll ask her and see."

"If she calls," Kenny sneered.

The phone rang and Steve picked it up. It was Ira. "I got a guy out here in the lobby, jumping up and down, Chief. Says he's gotta see ya. Name's Katzmer . . , oh . . . *Dr.* Katzmer, he informs me. He's dressed like he's fighting Desert Storm."

"Bring him up," said Steve.

"Anything you say, Chief."

Steve hung up and left Ken in the office to make some calls.

Katzmer arrived shortly, dressed in Desert Storm camouflage clothes. He carried a duffel bag.

"What's up?" asked Steve.

"That flap of skin?" said Katzmer, letting the duffel bag sink to the floor beside him.

"Yes."

"I took it to my cytologist friend at the university and he analyzed it."

"Yes."

"It's human. The cells are dead, somehow, but functioning. He's happier than a pig in slop. I left the skin with him."

"What's with the duffel bag?"

"Well, you're going to get down to the bottom of this, right?"

"Yes."

"Well, I'm with you. And you may need what's in the bag. It's Witch's Needles—four sets. They're ancient and they'll work on the flying thing, too. I found reference to those flying things in the photocopies of *Das Fayden*. I brought it with me."

"Good," said Steve. "I hope you brought a toothbrush too because we've got a mission coming up to save a couple of our people.

"It all involves the Coven of the Dark Dream. And it's for real, Katz. For fucking, real." Briefly, Steve explained to Katzmer the events of the last twenty hours. "Are you still in?" he asked Katzmer after he had finished.

"I don't think I have a choice. If you don't kill that thing it might come back for me. I'm in. I'm in."

Steve clapped Katzmer on the back and then introduced him around and sat him down at Kay's desk and told him to keep on working on *Das Fayden.*

Katzmer taken care of for the time being, Steve padded down the aisle, and back to his office. Ken Anderson had regained his own office and Steve sat down and stared at the phone. "Come on, Molly," he said to himself. "Call." And then he thought what had he been thinking. He didn't have Thom's address but he had asked his friend at L.A.P.D. to run Thom's address. He picked up the phone and dialed and Nancy Ellis was in. Yes, she had run the license plate number, and she was swamped or she would have gotten right back to him.

"It's okay, Nancy," said Steve. "Let me have it now."

Steve wrote the full name down, Thomas Sloat Lusk, and he resided at One Oak Road, Hennington, California.

Steve thanked Nancy and hung up.

He stared at the paper and felt bile rise in

his mouth. He had sent Molly and the girls into the hands of the Coven of the Dark Dream.

How could he ever forgive himself if anything happened to them?

Steve dropped his chin down to his chest. "Shit-shit-shit," he said. Not only had he sent her into the enemy hands, he really didn't even know exactly where she was. In a place called Hennington. And the girls. They're so delicate, so fragile. Such good little souls.

And the Convergence was near. Anna Kleiber had said that.

For a moment, the image of Carlotta hung upside down, still dripping blood on the carpet below appeared in his head. And then the image of Molly, Daphne, and Penny hung like that, and the pain welled up in him so fast that he choked back tears and finally let them flow. He cried for a few seconds and then he stopped himself.

Not doing them any good, he thought.

He stood up, grabbed a tissue and blew his nose. Then he sat back down and made his plans for rescuing the woman he loved.

He had but one small problem: he didn't know exactly where she was.

Twenty-two

KAY

The cell that Kay shivered in was just off Lady Eva's chambers. From here she was able to hear most of what went on within Lady Eva's private quarters.

She had not been fed or had water since those heinous things, Cutter and Radd, had raped her into unconsciousness.

They had not touched her since then. She had awakened in this limestone cell with only a blanket as company.

Her stomach growled and she spent a lot of time with her mouth and tongue pressed to the cool limestone walls, trying to trick her into sensing that water was going down her gullet.

When she was granted brief respites from consciousness, she slept and dreamed of drinking water in an oasis in the desert, or eating food. One dream had her eating a Thanksgiving meal, and another of eating a three-scoop vanilla ice-cream cone. When she awoke the hunger pangs and thirsty feel were ten times more acute.

Now, she moaned, "Water. Water," as she heard the sliding-*hop* sound of some Hadesmorph passing through Lady Eva's chambers. A guard, she guessed. She believed that Lady Eva and Cutter and Radd had been gone now for a day or two. She heard nothing of them.

She cried out for water and risked being raped, because she was just that thirsty, and because it seemed like a good gamble to her. It had come to her that nothing within these chambers happened without being ordered by Lady Eva. She was hoping getting water wasn't one of them. "Water," she croaked, now, her throat was so parched.

The sliding-*hop* sound stopped for a moment, then proceeded on its way.

Great, thought Kay, and if she'd had water enough to cry she would have. Instead she lay down and pressed her face against the cool floor and slept.

She awoke from a dream of drinking blood from a clear tumbler to the reality of being dragged out of the cell by her hair. She reached up and grabbed the Hadesmorph's wrist and pulled up to relieve the pain in her scalp.

Her body scraped against the floor and was partially draped by the thing's right wing. The stench of rotting flesh filled her nose, as she took the ride into Lady Eva's chambers.

"Pick her up, stupid."

It was the voice of Lady Eva. Kay did not see her at first. Suddenly she felt herself being lifted up at the waist and she saw Lady Eva, standing nude except for a bejeweled gold belt around her middle. On her head she wore a gold jeweled tiara, and in her hand she gripped a razor-sharp knife.

The thing plopped down in the center of a smooth man-made depression cut out of the limestone floor. It was located in the center of the room, at the middle of a giant pentagram inlaid in white marble in the limestone floor.

"Stay there," said Lady Eva, and it was more than a command. Kay felt her body paralyzed.

She was able to move her head. She lifted it and saw Cutter and Radd dragging in cast-iron stands, five of them. They placed them at the tips of each angle of pentagram. A four-foot long silver gutter was attached to each stand under a hammered out large silver bowl that was fastened to the top. The fancy guttering extended out over the depression that Kay was laying in.

Lady Eva smiled at her. "It takes a great deal of baby essence to bring a Hadesmorph into this world."

From the shadows came five naked women carrying wicker baskets with swaddling clothes. From one basket a baby started crying. Another started up in a piercing wail. And soon all were crying.

"They sent someone after you," said Lady Eva, "a man. We caught him, too. But soon it won't matter. After tomorrow night I will be too powerful for anyone to stop."

The witch pointed at her. "But you will be honored. I will spend much blood on you. These creatures can be made in any form I wish. And I have a special choice for you, and for the other they sent."

"Don't hurt the babies," Kay managed to say. "It's ungodly what you do. Please don't hurt them."

Lady Eva appeared not to hear. "You are to be honored today. It takes much baby essence to make a Hadesmorph," she said, having to almost scream to be heard over the babies. "You are the first of two today. The second spy they sent will be the other. All for the glory of Satan." She waved the women with the wicker baskets forward. They obeyed and placed the infants into the silver bowls.

Lady Eva began to chant strange incantations as her followers lit incense and begin to dance around the pentagram swinging censers as they cavorted.

Lady Eva finished her incantation and stepped up to the middle angle of the star. She took a stance with her legs spread far apart and her hands, gripping the anthame, the witch's knife, held high above the silver bowl in an unholy arch.

Kay closed her eyes and turned her head so she wouldn't see, and soon the unspeakable happened. She heard the wicked wet stabbing sounds, and the wail of the infant, and then the dreadful silence. And in seconds she felt the warm splatter of the baby's blood on her face.

Lady Eva danced to the next stand, as Kay screamed and screamed, until she had screamed herself into unconsciousness. And when she awoke, she would do anything for the Lady Eva, anything at all.

Twenty-three

STEVE AND MERRILEE

Steve bent over the conference-room table and spread a map. "I want to warn you guys up front that this is a tough one, and that it may have legal ramifications once it's over."

"There are always legal ramifications when the action's good," said Pauletti with a smirk on his face. The group grinned and murmured agreement.

Steve looked up and the twenty-one men and women around him continued to look among themselves and mumble. Steve cleared his throat and they looked back at him. No one dropped out. Not these guys. They were loyal people, and, loyal, greedy people (Steve had given them each a promise of a five-thousand-dollar bonus).

"Good," said Steve. "I guess I can still pick 'em right."

"Pay 'em right," said Paoletti, "they'll follow you anywhere."

The room broke into laughter.

Katzmer smiled too. Steve had hired him as technical consultant on the project, bonus in effect, also.

"Okay, our big problem is that we cannot use the authorities at all. If we do, our hostages will be killed immediately, I can guarantee it . . ."

Steve began briefing the group, leaving out the part about what he now believed or witnessed. What he did tell them was that some kind of weird animals seemed to be involved that could fly and were trained to kill. "So just deal with them as best you can, but don't get stymied because they're there," he told them. "The main thing is to find the Caverns because most likely these weirdos will be holding our hostages there. We don't know where the Caverns are, exactly, but as soon as we find them, the better off we will be."

As for the rest of the plan, it was simple. A few people go there undercover as a small group, with the others down the mountain, minutes away. The group scours the town, a second small group would cover the back road in, a third group on the road up.

There would be two radio-directional finder teams, and everyone would be wired. When something popped up they would all be called into play.

When finished, Steve stood up and joked, "One advantage of owning a security business, is you've got your own army at your beck and call."

"For a five-thousand-dollar bonus," said Munoz, "I'll beck and call all you want."

The group started to laugh again, but the door opened and Agnes stuck her head in. "It's for you, Steve. A Merrilee. She says it's important."

Steve hesitated a split second, then went to his office to answer the call.

"Steve, you sweet thing," she said, and Steve winced a little bit, remembering her come-ons at the party.

"Hi, Merrilee . . ." Steve started to say, but she interrupted.

"I have an invitation for you, and I will *not* take *No* for an answer. Do you understand?"

"Merrilee, I'm very busy right now. I did . . ."

"No excuses, Steve. Not this time. You're still interested in the Coven of the Dark Dream aren't you—that *Das Fayden* and all that nonsense? Aren't you?"

"Yes, I am," said Steve. He would just let her blow off steam, ask her a few questions he had and hang up.

"Okay then. I went to a lot of trouble, but I vouchsafed you to actually see the Dark Coven in celebration. Now, I will not take *No* for an answer. Do you understand?"

Steve thought a moment. Could he be this lucky? Maybe God was on his side. "Where will this take place, Merrilee?"

"Now don't say you won't come. You don't know how I had to beg and cajole to get permission. It's a bit of a drive. It's in a place called Hennington. Do you know it?"

"No," said Steve, hearing himself lie. "Where is it?"

"It's in the mountains. A lovely drive and it's wonderful. Smells of fresh air and everything."

"Do we go to someone's house there, or what, for the ceremony?"

"Don't worry. Just come up here. I'm staying at a friend's cabin. I want you to come up and stay the night."

"Are you sure there's room?"

"Plenty of room. You just come up."

"Okay, Merrilee. But where will the ceremony be?"

"Why is that important?"

"Because I want to know whether to wear nice clothes, or not?"

"Warm clothes, Steve. It's at a place they call the Caverns up here. And the ceremony is at midnight, so wear warm clothes."

Steve pressed the phone against his ear tightly and leaned over to grab a pencil and piece of paper. "Okay, Merrilee, tell me how to get to you."

"You owe me," she said with a lilt of joy in her voice, and then proceeded to give him the directions to her cabin in Hennington, California.

Twenty-four

TO THE CAVERNS

Steve turned off the Interstate Five and headed inland toward the mountains and Hennington.

One communications van, disguised as a camper had preceded him by twenty minutes and one was following perhaps a ten-minute drive at high speed behind.

Things had changed a little with Merrilee's call. It was a great stroke of luck. It would allow Steve time to find out where the Caverns were located while his people got ready down below.

He put Ken Anderson in charge of the field force while he was in the company of Merrilee.

He had made Katzmer the control for this operation. He telephoned Senator Dest and informed her of what had happened to Carlotta Chalmers and her family. The news had already made the TV, and he knew that Senator Dest would have more clout than any one he had

240

contact with when it came to pulling the authorities in on this.

Steve introduced Katzmer to the senator by the phone, and she said that she was flying down immediately. Knowing her affection for Carlotta, he tested her by phone and then had made the decision to trust her on this matter. She would hook up with Katzmer when she got down here and he would explain everything to her. She promised Steve not to do anything on her own until she had the complete story as relayed by Katzmer.

As Steve talked to her he was surprised at her willingness to help. "I thought it would be tougher convincing you," he told her.

The senator said nothing for a moment, then, in voice choked with emotion, "I owe Carlotta everything; she was my friend; she believed in me when I didn't even believe in myself, Steve."

"Good," said Steve. "Then you want these bastards as bad as I do."

"Enough to risk my political career and my life, Steve. We must get Molly and the girls back."

Steve wondered how much she knew about Carlotta. "Do you know about Lady May?" he asked.

"Oh, Steve. Of course I knew Carlotta was Lady May. I've danced with her in the Circle of the Crystal Moon. What I can't figure out is how we could have been caught so unaware."

"Then you know of the Dark Coven."

"Of course."

"The Good Coven got taken because they got outsmarted," said Steve. "Up until recently, Carlotta thought that the Dark Coven had perished with her sister, Jobina. You guys just had your guard down. That was the problem."

"It's not supposed to happen like that."

"Well it did."

"I'll be on the next plane."

"I'll be on my way to Hennington by then," he said, then said good-bye and hung up.

Steve hit the base of the mountain about seven o'clock. He wasn't sure how long it would take him to get up the hill, but within ten minutes he'd passed the disguised radio van that had been ahead of him. They carried four men each and weapons. Paoletti was a demolition expert and had packed in all kinds of explosives, not to mention a Vietnam War vintage flamethrower. "Flaming gases for the masses," he had chortled, when loading it on board.

Katzmer had brought eight of the long "Witch Needles" that looked like ancient Spanish stilettos. He had passed them out judiciously. The needles' metal was a cast-iron silver alloy, and was blessed by the church. Poke a witch in the abdomen, specifically in the heart, and she was dead—or so was the legend.

Steve carried one, the scabbard taped to the side of his lower right leg. Some of the men had been skeptical, and he'd told them simply that even if they did not believe that they worked, the witches did and would be afraid of them. He left out the part about how he had seen the white witches fly for fear of creating a credibility problem.

In half an hour, he had reached the town of Hennington, with its one gas station, one market, and one diner, and passed through it the way Merrilee had directed, and a mile out of town turned down a dirt road. The smell of pine was sweet in Steve's nose, and the drop in temperature refreshing.

Within a minute he pulled up in front of a sprawling one-storey cabin. He was wired with a one-way bug. The vans could hear him, but he could receive any communications from them. He wore a directional transmitter taped to the small of his back.

He wondered if the vans had made it up the hill enough to hear him. "I'm at the cabin," he said out loud, and opened the car door. "You guys remember. Tomorrow is the big ceremony. We gotta get it done by then or it's too late." That had been what Katzmer had told him. It would be at the Convergence that Daphne would be sacrificed in the name of all that was unholy—he'd read it in his photocopy of *Das Fayden*.

The cabin door opened and Merrilee came out. She was dressed in jeans and a tight sweater, her hair was a helmet crown of blond hair that would rival one of Dolly Parton's wigs.

"Come on up," she said.

He got his bag out of the back seat. He'd put it there instead of in the trunk because his weapons were in the trunk and he didn't want to risk Merrilee seeing them.

Merrilee breezed down the steps, threw her arms around him and gave him a big hug. Her breasts pressed into him and he staggered back with the impact of her gesture. She kissed him full on the lips. Reflex kicked in and he sort of kissed her back, but he had no idea why. She pulled away and smiled. "You can do better than that," she giggled. "Or I'm not female."

Steve laughed to be polite, but wondered what kind of night he was going to have. He didn't want Merrilee in any way but perhaps a friendship. He liked Molly.

Oh, well. It's going to be an interesting evening.

She looped her arm through his, and guided him toward the cabin. She took him to her bedroom and pointed to the bed. "Here is where we sleep," she said. "You can hang up your clothes in the closet.

Steve started to protest.

"There's only one bed," she said. "And we have to share it. There's no choice, and no objection on my part. Are you gay or something?"

"No," said Steve, "it's not that. It's just that

we barely know each other, and there's AIDS to worry about, and everything else."

"I don't have AIDS." She looked appalled at the thought.

"I didn't say you did. But I haven't been tested since my last relationship, and I wasn't expecting this."

Merrilee sat on the bed. "I have protection if you don't."

She's a nympho, thought Steve. "Look, I don't know you well enough. I can sleep on the couch until we get to know each other. How about that?"

Merrilee hopped off the bed and pointed a wicked index finger at him. "If my name were Molly you'd be in the sack with me, I'll bet."

Steve was speechless.

Merrilee continued, "You think I didn't notice how you kept looking at her while you were dancing with *me*. It was very rude."

And I'm in a lot of trouble, here, thought Steve. But, I need her help. Maybe, I should do it.

He knew that among his male friends, none would believe that he would hesitate, but the truth was that something about her bothered him. Being so fucking forward the least of it.

Steve bucked up his courage and smiled sweetly. "You're very beautiful, Merrilee. And, yes, I do like Molly a lot. But if you just slow down and give me a chance, maybe I can like you a lot too. After all, we've only just met."

Merrilee glared at him for a moment then twirled and walked toward the bathroom. "I got to go to the Caverns today, Steve. They're magnificent. That's where the ceremony will be performed."

"Can we go take a look?" he said. "Then I'll take you out in the woods and we'll make love. I've got a sleeping bag that'll keep us warm as toast."

Okay, it's a shitty thing to do, he thought, lying to her like that.

"Is that a promise?"

"Yes," said Steve.

"It's dark, you won't be able to see much."

"Maybe they'll let us inside."

"I doubt it, but if you'll keep your promise . . . ?"

"I'll keep it."

"You'll be glad you did." She walked over to the closet and reached in and pulled out two long robes. "It is the attire required by all who enter Cavern of the Dark Dream," she said, and then giggled. "I got one for you."

Merrilee stripped down to her matching black panties and bra and threw on her brown robe. Steve tossed his over his clothes. "Aren't you going to be cold in that?" he asked.

She smiled. "I'm hot all over. Can't you tell that?"

Steve laughed. "Yes, I can."

He donned his brown robe, and found it warm and roomy.

246

They took his car and drove back through town. He knew that by now the communication vans were in place and he would be tracked. This was the break they were looking for. Once he had reached the Caverns they would get a fix and then radio down the hill for the support teams to come up, and then they would plan and execute the assault on the Caverns, and rescue their people if they could.

"Another mile or so out of town," Merrilee said. "There's a turn-off to the left. I'll tell you when."

They reached the turnoff, and Steve drove for a half a mile, before being stopped by robed men with assault rifles.

Steve looked ahead and there were at least a hundred cars parked in the meadow.

"What do you want?" one robed man asked. He was no-nonsense about it. "You're not of the order."

Merrilee leaned across him and said, "He's with me. I'm Merrilee. I've been invited."

Steve saw a look of shock scroll across his face. He nodded, like he was confused. "Yes, My Lady."

"I'm not your *Lady*. I'm a liberated woman and I'm going to report your rudeness. Do you hear me?"

The orange-robed guard backed away. "Yes, My . . . yes," he said. He waved Steve and Merrilee on through.

"Put some fire in his pants, didn't I," said Merrilee proudly.

"You sure did," said Steve, and the gig was up, now. That man not only knew her, he was frightened of her. Steve would bet his life on it. His heart began to beat a little faster. "Where to?" he asked and wasn't surprised when she pointed up to a stand of trees. "Is that where the Caverns are?" he asked.

"Yes," she said. "You can park next to those two vans there. The ones with all the antennas on them."

Steve stared in shock. Parked next to the trees were his two communication vans. He looked in his rearview mirror and saw three jeeps behind carrying three guards each. There was no escape.

Steve said, "So you used the book writing as a cover to move around in the occult world . . . is that how it works, Lady Eva?"

"Bravo," said Lady Eva. "You're a smart one you are."

"Not smart enough. You got me."

"I've had this planned out for a long time, Steve. Don't feel bad. And I really do like you."

Steve thought immediately of the witch needle taped to his leg. But it was too late. He brought the car to a stop beside the vans. His door was jerked opened from the outside and he was pulled from his seat by a robed man the size of a mountain. Steve was slammed against the side of the car.

"Careful, Bork," said Lady Eva, who had just

exited the car. "I want him fresh. Take him and put him with the others."

Steve did not resist.

Twenty-five

LOVERS

Molly clutched the two girls close to her on the tiny bed in the cell. She wasn't sure how long they had been held prisoner—a day, maybe two.

The children and she were taken out to exercise once in the hall, and then been fed a decent meal. The guard had not answered any of her questions, he had simply given them orders, brought the food, and watched them while they were exercising. Other than that they had been left alone.

Occasionally she thought of Sloat's vile hands on her, how cold his touch had been—and he had touched everywhere with his fingers. But he had done nothing else. Once they had reached the Caverns, he turned them over to the guards, who had dragged them down inside the Caverns past the meeting area into Lady Eva's chambers—and beyond, to the cells where they were kept prisoners.

"Mommy," said Daphne. "Why are they doing this?"

"Because they are evil, Daphne. They are what we taught you to be wary of—they are the Coven of the Dark Dream."

"Well, let's kill them, and get away then."

"If we can, we will, Daphne. But it doesn't look good. Part of the ritual they will perform will involve you. They will give you a liquid to drink. It will be vile smelling, but drink it anyway, because it will lessen the pain—it's a narcotic sort of. So you won't suffer much."

"She won't put the narcotic in it," said Daphne. "What I do drink will make me obey. I read the Bad Lady's mind. She is going to make it as painful as possible for me so it'll hurt you more." She stuck out her lip. "If I could kill her I would."

It bothered Molly to hear her daughter speak like that, but she remembered Steve's words about war footing. She told Daphne, "Get away if you can. Kill if you have to." She looked at Penny, and said, "And you too, sweetheart. Just get away if you can."

A noise interrupted their conversation and Molly heard the big bastard who had pushed her around when she first came in, say, "Over there, shit-for-brains." Suddenly Steve was sprawled out in front of their cell. A massive hand reached down and picked him up and dragged him to the cell opposite them. "Ah, yes," said Bork, the Keeper of the Cavern. He ran his hands over

251

Steve's body. "Ah-hah! What's this," he said. He pulled up Steve's pant leg and ripped off a knife of some kind. "Witch needle!" exclaimed Bork. "Well, I'll be damned. I oughta ram this up your arse." He pushed Steve into the cell and shut the barred door, and locked it with a big jailor's key. "That oughta keep ya," he said and stomped off.

"Steve," she whispered across the eight feet to his cell. "Steve, are you okay?"

She heard him moan and gradually he began to move. He fumbled for the wall and managed to sit up and face her. Blood was trickling from his forehead. "Merrilee is Lady Eva," he said to her.

"Yes, we know. How badly are you hurt?"

"I'm okay. I tried to fight him, but he's so damn big."

"Yes. He is. Listen, y'know Thom, that's Lady Eva's son."

"Oh great. We're really screwed. They've rounded up all the people that I brought up here to help rescue you. I've got people down the mountain, but they're only coming up if we don't straighten things out before the ceremony, tomorrow night.

"They will miss the radio traffic from up here, but I don't know what they'll do about it. Never thought they'd pick us all up at once. The good news is that we have time before that Convergence thing. Maybe we can figure something out."

"I don't know," said Molly. "I think we're finished, speaking realistically."

252

Steve nodded at her, and then Lady Eva strode in, and looked at Molly. "I don't know what he sees in you, when he can have me. But I do know that Steve will be mine, and you will be made to suffer if not." Lady Eva backed away and pointed to Steve. "I could *enchant* you into doing it, but it's much too easy that way."

Lady Eva motioned and from the other room Bork appeared. She held out her hand. Bork slapped the witch needle in it. "You came to kill me, Steve." She motioned to Bork to open Molly's cell. He did so.

"Pull the sow out."

Bork reached in and brought Molly out with a grunt. He pushed the girls back in as they tried to go with her. The girls started screaming.

Lady Eva walked around Molly flicking at her with the witch needle, then said to Bork, "Get him out, too."

Bork obeyed, and then Lady Eva led them deeper down the tunnel. It twisted and turned and they came out on an outcropping of limestone over pitch black pit. A carrion stench arose from the darkness that was overpowering. Lady Eva said, "Lights!" Bork found some hidden switch and flipped it, lighting the pit.

"Oh, no," Molly said in disgust.

"Shit," said Steve.

Lady Eva said, "Bat guano, and drippings from the cave springs. Not a lot, just enough to make it sticky. Have a good look."

Lady Eva grabbed Molly and pushed her to

the edge. Molly saw the bones and half-devoured remains of human beings. A man right below her moaned with pain. "He's still alive."

"Yes, he is, isn't he?" said Lady Eva.

"Takes weeks to die that way," said Bork.

"What's that on him?" asked Molly. "It looks like it's moving."

"Those are bugs and cockroaches," explained Lady Eva. "He's too weak to move. He's stuck in the shit. And the bugs are eating him alive. It's a horrible way to die, don't you agree?" With this she pushed Molly slightly forward.

Molly screamed and backed up from the pit.

"Do you like it, Steve?"

"It's disgusting?"

"I agree. Now, Molly, show Steve how loyal you are to him. Would you rather he favor me with his manhood in bed, or would you rather I push you in the pit?"

Molly's heart raced. She looked at Steve and he saved her the embarrassment of saving herself. He said, "Manhood, of course, Molly."

Her voice quivered as she spoke. "Manhood," she said.

"Ah," said Lady Eva, "now we've come to an understanding." She looked at Bork. "Return her to her children."

Bork grabbed her and pushed her back into the tunnel and led her to her cell. The last thing she had heard Lady Eva say was directed to Steve. She had said, "We make a game of the pit. We push our victims in. The fall breaks a few of their bones, and then we bet on how long they last. That man down there might set a record. Molly, though, I'd lower her down so she could run around in that shit, but never get out. It would take her a very long time to die. Don't forget that, Steve."

"I won't," Steve had said. "I won't forget anything you've said."

"Where's Mommy?" Penny asked fearfully.

Daphne scooted over to her and put her arm around her little sister. "Shoosh, Penny-Peanut. Mommy's off with the Bad Lady and Mr. Brogan." She felt Penny's arms encircle her, and squeeze.

She looked out through the bars at the opposite cell. "I wanna go home," said Penny. "I wanna see Grandma Lottie, and Motu, and everybody, I miss my dollies, too."

Daphne hugged her a little and said, "Don't worry, Penny-Peanut. We'll be home soon. Mommy'll get us out of here."

"I want Mommy," Penny whined, and it made Daphne angry—not at Penny, but at that Bad Lady who had taken them and that Thom.

"Thom-the-Bomb is a bad man, and he's going to be punished. So will that Bad Lady, Penny."

"Are they going to hurt us, Duffy?"

"I won't let them hurt you, Penny. I'll protect you, so don't be afraid."

The sound of footsteps preceded them and the mean big fat old guy in the orange robe brought Mommy back, opened the cell door, and shoved her in.

"Don't you hurt my Mommy!" Penny-Peanut screamed.

"Sh!" said Daphne.

"I'm okay," Molly said, but Daphne heard the shaking in her mother's voice, and felt her trembling as Daphne and Penny both hugged her at once.

The big man leaned in close and stuck his fat moon-face up to the bars. He stared at her with big brown eyes. "BOO!" he said.

Penny screamed, but Daphne did not. She glared at him, carefully studying his face. "I hate you," she said in a normal tone of voice. She locked onto his eyes with hers and she stared at him coldly. She repeated to herself: "I hate you."

The big Bork guy closed his eyes suddenly, stood up, and glanced back at Daphne. She kept her eyes on his. He turned roughly away and walked on down the hall.

"That's telling him, sweetie," said her mommy, her voice still shaking.

"Where's Mr. Brogan?" asked Penny. She nuzzled against Mommy's breast.

Daphne felt her mommy's body tense up. "I don't know," Mommy said. "With the Dark Queen."

"The witch," said Penny with fearful awe in her voice.

"The wicked witch," Daphne told her, and saw a picture in her head of the Bad Lady in her head, with Mr. Brogan. "Mommy, I can see them in my mind."

"Who, honey?"

"Mr. Brogan and the Bad Witch Lady."

"Mommy, they're *naked*."

"Stop seeing that. Think of something else."

Daphne tried, but the image persisted. "I can't, Mommy. I can't. The picture won't go away."

"I can see it now, too, Mommy," said Penny. "Stop sharing it, Daphne."

"I'm not sharing it at all," said Daphne.

"I can see it, too, girls," said Molly. "Try and shut it out."

Daphne tried and tried in vain, but couldn't make the image go away.

"It's the witch," Daphne said, the moment she realized it. "She's sharing it, just to be mean." Daphne was not sure how she knew, but she was sure she was right.

"What's that thing, Mommy?" asked Penny-Peanut. "OOH! What are they doing, Mommy? Why is he kissing her pee-pee? Hunh? Why are they doing that?"

As Bork took Molly back to the cells, Steve eyed Lady Eva, then the cavernous pit less than four feet away. He decided to toss her in, let her crash onto the rocks below, and lay in that crap down there. He would run after and kill Bork, release the children and somehow get them out of here. Anything would be better than letting this woman continue with her mad plans.

"Let me ask you one question," he said to Lady Eva. "Why are you going to all the trouble to get me in bed? I'm not that good, really. And besides, I came here to stop you."

"Kill me, you mean," she said with a wide smile on her face. She touched his forearm lightly. "You intrigue me. You're handsome. You're not that attracted to me—my sexual magnetism reaches out to both sexes, males in particular. But not to you." She pointed around the cavern with her free hand. "And even in here, where my power is the strongest, I still can't read your mind."

"Thank God for that," he said, and quickly ducked down, grabbing her arm as he did so. He bolted forward with a step, scooped her, and tossed her over the lip of the cliff.

He watched as Lady Eva's robe fluttered as she dropped about four feet down the shaft, then righted herself in midair. She had not screamed. Her body was limned in green light as she floated level with the cliff's lip. She laughed. "You disappoint me, Steve. Did you forget that I'm a witch, and I am on my own consecrated ground?" She smiled sweetly as she floated up to the cliff's edge, and over to Steve and settled down next to him. The green light disappeared from her silhouette. "I should punish Molly, or perhaps Penny. Oh yes, I'll surprise you.

"Oh, and by the way, if you try to kill me again: first, you will fail, for now I am protected; and second, I will skin Molly alive in front of your very eyes, and make you eat her raw flesh." Her words were made the more chilling by the sweet smile that accompanied them. Steve believed that she meant every word of her threat.

He nodded in understanding.

"Good," she said. "Now perhaps we can have some fun. Let me give you a brief tour back here, and then off to some fun and relaxation, huh?" Lady Eva tucked her arm in his, and started guiding him toward a different tunnel than the one that Molly and Bork had disappeared down. "Please don't try anything, Steve. It does hurt my feelings, believe it or not, that you won't even give me a chance." She pouted like a little kid, looked him square in the eyes and feigned an anguished expression on her face.

Steve snorted, "After the Convergence tomorrow night, you're going to kill us all anyway? So, what's the difference?"

"No. I am not going to kill you, I'm going to stud you for my pleasure." She pooched up her lips and made a kissing sound. "In time you're going to like it very much. I'm tough, but very fair. And our children will need their father . . ."

"And Molly and the girls?" he asked.

"After a while you'll come to love me and that's all that matters."

Steve felt a wave of powerlessness flood through him. He matched steps with Lady Eva.

She took him another way back to her bedchamber. "There are miles and miles of caves and tunnels here, Steve," she said pointing to off-shoot tunnels. "This one leads to my private entrance and exit to the caverns. It opens out on a luxurious meadow, where I love to walk." She looked up at him with rapt attention. "Maybe we'll make love out there, one night, under the stars. Would you like that? Being outside, I mean?"

"Yes, I would love to be outside," Steve said, the true meaning of his words only thinly veiled in his tone.

"Now, don't be like that, silly," she said like a schoolgirl. She stopped and turned to face him. "What if I promise not to kill Molly, or hurt her. Will you cheer up, then? Hunh?"

Steve searched her face for some trick. Her blue eyes engulfed him. "Well," he said, "and the girls, too?"

"That depends, Steve. If you make our first time, a wonderful time for me. If you really try to please me. If you relax and give yourself to me wholeheartedly, I will spare the girls, too."

"What about the Convergence. You have to sacrifice . . ."

Lady Eva raised both her hands. *"Symbolically*

sacrifice, Steve. Not truly blood sacrifice the girl. After all she is the Virgin Child, or virgin birth. That must be respected." She gazed meaningfully into his eyes. "You see, I'm not as big a monster, as these Crystal Moon prissies have made me out to be."

Steve felt the uncomfortable mantle of uncertainty wrap its chilling fabric around his mind. There was nothing *symbolic* about any of this horrid woman, and still, if there were a chance she was telling the truth, he would cooperate.

"Okay," he said with as much feeling as he could muster. "As long as they're not harmed, I'll go along with it."

"Good. You won't be sorry. I promise, I *will* please you."

She led him back to her bedchamber, and stripped naked before him. "Take your clothes off," she said.

He complied, piling his garments in a heap at his feet.

"Now," she said, and Steve watched her shudder in anticipation. Her voice wavered with lust as she continued. "Get on your hands and knees. Kiss my feet, and lick your way up . . . okay, Steve?"

Steve ignored her ruse of submission: "Okay, Steve," as if he had a choice. He dropped to his knees and did as he was told.

After his third time, Steve rolled off Lady

261

Eva, and lay back on the giant black silk sheets, and sighed.

Lady Eva got out of bed. "Wonderful! Wonderful!" She stood naked by the bed and pointed at him and said again with glee, "Wonderful! Now, I must get bathed and dressed."

Steve sat up and watched her. She stepped into an open showering area that had been carved out of the cavern wall. She reached out and turned on the faucet, adjusted the water and began to bathe herself. Her long hair became wet quickly and hung in stringy ropes down her milk-white body. Her large breasts had a buoyancy of their own, they bounced and jiggled rhythmically to her motions.

Steve looked away and thought about his situation. He knew that the longer he waited, the longer he and Molly and the girls were alive, the better the chances of being rescued by Katzmer and the others. They had until tomorrow night at the time of the Convergence before things would truly turn to shit, and Steve would find out whether Lady Eva was lying to him. That was enough time for Katzmer and the crew to find them and rescue them, with outside agencies this time. Senator Dest would make sure they cooperated, especially when the whole first wave was discovered to have disappeared.

Lady Eva stepped from the shower stall and grabbed a towel that hung from a wooden ring. She dried herself and signaled him to come over. She took a hair drier and a brush from a small mirrored dressing table and waited until he trotted over in his nakedness.

She handed the drier and brush to him, and he started to brushing and drying out her hair.

"We must be clean," she said, "for the Convergence Ceremony. For my Becoming Ceremony."

"What time tomorrow night is it?" Steve asked.

Lady Eva laughed a schoolgirl's laugh. "Oh, Steve," she said. "You're such an innocent one. So easily fooled."

Steve brought the brush up to the back of her head, caught up a large mass of hair in the bristles and pulled out and gasped. Two shirt-button sized, sentient blue eyes stared up at him from two small eye sockets in the back of Lady Eva's skull. They studied him carefully from behind the tangled black mass that was her hair.

"You see, Steve," she said. "The Convergence is tonight; or should I say in the early morning—3:00 A.M. Just two and a half hours away." One of the small eyes winked at him. "And we have much to do, my lover. My man. My Steve. First of which is to prepare the girls for sacrifice—human sacrifice. All of this that our Father has given us is based on blood, babies' blood. The Blood Cycle is now. It is the Season of Blood. It is the Season of the Witch!"

Twenty-six

RESCUERS

Katzmer was worried about Steve and the others. There had been no communication from them after the first hour and a half that they were on the mountain.

"Has the senator checked in, yet?" he asked the blond-haired young man in front of the communication console.

Katzmer went back to perusing the photocopies of the *Das Fayden* he was translating. A new and deadly wrinkle had developed in this nightmare. He would go over it with the senator when she arrived.

Katzmer took a sip of coffee and reflected on his involvement so far. For the most part he was excited with the project. After all, the odds of being embroiled in an adventure when you were a museum curator were pretty damn slim and now he was up to his documents in matters of life and death, not to mention an event of historical importance.

Taking charge had been easy. His training in the Israeli military had kicked in as soon as Steve had come forward and asked him to be "control." He grasped the concept immediately. It was like an insurance policy that kicks in if things went bad.

Now, Katzmer sat in an unmarked motor coach backup command center. They were parked three miles from the base of the mountains up which the first team had driven, and promptly disappeared.

Denise, his personal guard, stepped up to the door and said, "I see lights."

Todd, the radio operator, twisted around and told Katzmer, "The senator's chopper's coming in."

Katzmer exited the motor coach in time to see two more of Steve's men jump from a truck and lay down flares on the side road. One man used two flashlights to guide the chopper down.

Senator Dest, a large briefcase in one hand, hopped off the chopper and ran hunched-over towards Katzmer.

"Senator," he said, taking her offered hand briefly. "We've got a problem already."

"What kind of a problem?" she asked as they hurried toward the motor coach.

"We've lost all contact with the advance team." He held the door for the senator. She climbed up and into the coach and he guided her immediately to a well-lit situation aboard.

Katzmer continued, "We sent in two unmarked communication trucks and four unmarked cars with a total of twelve men and women in them. They've all disappeared. No transmission."

"So why haven't you gone after them with the rest of your people?" she asked.

Katzmer shrugged. "We *are* the rest of the people. Steve didn't want to involve the authorities because of the credibility factor—covens, witches, et cetera. He said we would use you for that." Katzmer went on to explain the entire situation to her. He included that Molly was involved, and that Daphne and Penny's lives were in danger. "I think that they will be safe until the Convergence, which we thought was tomorrow night. But there's a hitch."

The senator's face looked grim. "What's that," she said.

Katzmer guided her back past the communications bank to a table with photocopies of *Das Fayden* on it.

"This book is the one with all the answers," he said. "I've been working on the translation and I've come to an interesting part about the Convergence."

"Yes," said Senator Dest.

"It says here that the sacrifices are made on this night, not tomorrow night like we thought. The *essence*—a blood product is then used for the next day in honor of the Convergence. It means that the shit hits the fan tonight. And we're in trouble because we don't have anyone to send up there."

Katzmer shut up and let the message sink in. He was not sure of the senator's involvement in the scheme of things, but he knew Steve had a great deal of faith in her political savvy.

"Get me a cup of coffee," she said. "And a telephone."

Katzmer nodded to Todd, and Todd got up and went to the coffee pot, and poured a cup of coffee, brought it over and set it down.

"Okay," she said. She opened her briefcase and pulled out a personal telephone book. "How much time do we have?"

"Maybe three hours, maybe two. I'm not sure. Most rituals are midnight rites, but the *Das Fayden* says three phases past midnight—a phase equates to about an hour, I think, but it could be a shorter period of time."

Senator Dest opened her address book. "I have my other people coming by car." She looked at Katzmer. "I never told Steve this, but Daphne and Penny both have the middle name Veronica. They are named after me. And I'll be damned if I'll let some madwoman get away with murdering them."

She dialed her first number, and Katzmer reflected that Steve had been right in his judgment of Senator Veronica Dest.

Twenty-seven

THE CONVERGENCE

Under Lady Eva's orders, Bork escorted Steve back to his cell. Steve was still in shock at seeing (and being seen by) Lady Eva's rear set of eyes.

When he discovered them, Lady Eva had turned around. She had smiled and said, "There are prices to pay for everything, my dear Steve. The corruption of my body is one such price. The same power that makes me beautiful despite my years, makes anomalies of my body."

Steve had wanted to ask her if she had any more he should know about, but found himself speechless as an image of those small eyes gazing at him came into his mind.

Bork shoved him into his cell, and then trudged off. Molly, Daphne and Penny sat staring at him with chagrined looks on their faces.

"What?" he asked.

"Never mind," said Molly. "It's not important, now."

Steve shook off his need to probe further and said, *"We* are in deeper than I thought."

Molly gave him a puzzled look. "We're in about as deep as we can get," she said.

"No. The Convergence is tonight, not tomorrow night."

"What?!" Molly gripped the cell bars and pressed her face between them. "That means they'll come for . . ."

"Molly! Isn't there anything you can do? I saw you float in midair; I saw Lady Eva float in midair, too. Isn't there something you can do? You're a witch, too."

"Steve, our Coven doesn't do this kind of thing. These hideous things. Carlotta was the last to practice counter magic. She was the one who levitated all of us at the party."

Steve said, "Look, no matter what your religion teaches, there has to be something in it about defending yourself, and the girls."

Daphne snuggled close to Molly. "If I get the chance," Daphne said, "I'm going to bite that big Bork guy and claw his eyes out."

Penny whispered, "Someone's coming."

A man Steve had not seen before stopped in front of his cell. He was short with brown eyes and a balding head. He wore a blue-black silk robe. "My name is Kleiber. Dwight Kleiber. I am high priest for the Coven. Lady Eva has told me much of you. I must say, I approve. You are a fine specimen. Some of your men are fine specimens, too. They will serve us well." He turned and called, "Bork," and soon the giant man, dressed in a orange silk robe trudged into view. "Take the children."

Molly shoved the girls back behind her and stooped, leaning forward ready to fight. Steve involuntarily reached out from between the bars and tried to grab either one of the men, but he was too far away.

Bork laughed, and asked Kleiber, "Should I hurt the mother?"

"Just enough to get the children out."

Steve howled and again grabbed for Kleiber's robe, but his hand caught empty air. Kleiber glanced at him and sneered.

"It's okay, Mommy," said Daphne in such a quiet voice, so childlike and out of context of the life and death tension of the moment, that everyone stopped, frozen almost in midaction.

"It's okay, Mommy," Daphne said again. "Everything is going to be all right."

Steve saw Daphne take Penny's hand, and pull her from behind Molly. Molly moved to stop her, looking confused for a moment, then oddly, Steve thought, relaxed, and let her pass. Before moving, Daphne leaned over and kissed her on the cheek. "It's going to be all right, Mommy," she said, like she was soothing a child. She pulled Penny toward the cell gate and Molly did not try to stop her.

Bork opened the cell door and Daphne led Penny out.

Steve watched the two men escort the girls down the tunnel and as he looked over at Molly an image of Daphne's face appeared in his head. "It's okay, Mr. Brogan," the image said. "Grandma Lottie says it'll be okay."

But Carlotta is dead, thought Steve.

"Yes, she is, isn't she," said Daphne's image and then it disappeared.

Within minutes of taking the children Bork returned and tossed a pair of leg cuffs into Steve's cell. He turned and tossed a second pair into Molly's cell, and said, "Put them on."

Steve nodded to Molly and she attached the cuffs first around one ankle then on the other. Steve did the same. They were adequate for walking at a slow pace, but any pace above that would trip the wearer onto the floor.

Bork led them through the tunnel and through Lady Eva's chambers to the tunnel that gave out on the main tunnel to the large meeting cavern. Bork told them to wait and not move and he went ahead.

The distinct sound of human voices chanting wafted down to Steve and Molly. Steve told Molly about the image of Daphne that had appeared in his head and what it had said about Carlotta.

"I saw it, too," Molly said. "That's why I let

271

her go so easily, but I don't know what it means. I have been racking my brain trying to remember what I was taught as a young kid about the Coven of the Dark Dream. Just as Carlotta, Queen of the Coven o the Crystal Moon, held the real magical power, so does the Queen of the Coven of the Dark Dream—she's the one with the black magic. And this is her holy ground, this Cavern. If we can desecrate it in some major way it will lessen her strength."

Steve reached for this ray of hope. "How do we do that?"

Molly sighed. "Without ritual potions and implements, and Carlotta's power, not easily. It has to do with control, too. Right now, she is totally in control of her environment. If we can shake it up somehow, it will weaken her. But we have to do it before the Convergence. Afterwards, there will be no stopping her. She will be able to take on the armies of the world and they will perish in perdition's flames. For real, Steve. The legend speaks of a reign of a thousand years of Darkness, Death, and Fiery Destruction at the hands of the Queen of the Dark Dream."

Bork appeared up the tunnel and motioned them forward. Steve whispered to Molly, "I'm counting on you. You know more than I. Think of something I can do to disrupt Lady Eva's power."

"Steve," Molly whispered back, then went silent. She wrinkled up her nose at the stench.

Steve smelled it too and they looked behind

272

them. Molly crowded close to Steve at the hideous sight not ten feet away. "Winged Things," Steve said, staring at their long, sharp teeth. Their eyes were large, and filled with cunning. They slip-hopped along, dragging their wings beside them.

Steve heard Bork laugh. "Hurry, now, kiddies, before Cutter and Radd get hungry."

Steve clutched Molly and they hurried to catch up with Bork who guided them toward the meeting cavern. As they approached, the chanting became clearer and louder. Steve did not understand the words, but their rhythm was almost a narcotic, and sung by hundreds of voices.

As they reached the main cavern, Bork stepped aside and pushed them out at the side of the stage area of the natural amphitheater. Steve felt Molly's grip tighten on his arm as they faced at least three hundred people, stripped naked except for green leather thongs around their left thighs with silver bells attached. They were organized in groups of thirteen, and swayed in rhythm to their chant. At least one in each group wore a silver crown or tiara, and all sported silver necklaces with the charm of the Coven of the Dark Dream on them.

In front of the stage were piled the weapons Steve's men had brought, including Paolettis two flame throwers. His men stood shackled, and off to the side. They looked hang-dog tired. Paoletti looked at Steve and shrugged. Steve wondered where Ken Anderson was as he looked down the line of his people: Brandner, Paine, Lacher, Baker, Munoz, Black and Relling. Kay Audette. Lund and the others must be dead. Ken Anderson, dead? Shit.

Steve felt the depression of helpless rage. He was caught like an animal, and there was no way out, no way to avenge himself on her.

Lady Eva, dressed in a diaphanous black robe, with a silver jeweled crown, strode on stage and raised her hands. The multitudes ceased their chanting, and Lady Eva spoke: "Behold the army of the Crystal Moon," she said, indicating Steve's men with a sweep of her left arm. "And their weapons below." She moved her right arm to the pile of arms at the base of the stage. "And," she continued the motion of her right arm, "see the granddaughter of the Great Lady May, Queen of the Coven of the Crystal Moon, and the man she so wantonly tried to *steal* from your Queen."

A spontaneous roar of outrage rose up from the masses.

Lady Eva reveled in the deafening sound, then calmed them with a quick gesture of both hands raised up toward the cavern ceilings.

In the silence, Dwight Kleiber came forward and whispered in her ear. A smile crossed her face. She whispered back to him, and dismissed him. "It seems that other interlopers have come to harm us. As we celebrate here, they travel up our mountain in their pathetic cars and hover above, searching for our meeting with helicop-

274

ters. But fear not the interloper, for our Most Dark Holy of Businesses will be completed in a few minutes and then no force on earth will be able to stand against your Queen."

A cheer rose up and with a beating of drums, Steve watched Daphne, dressed in a silver robe, a red sash cinched tight around her waist, being escorted out by gold-robed women, and Penny followed, dressed in a white cotton gown.

Steve's view was broken by Dwight Kleiber who rushed over to Bork. "I'm sending Cutter and Radd up after the helicopters and I want you to put extra guards on the entrance. A precaution. Not to worry. In a few minutes, Our Queen will Converge and she will take the interlopers to their fiery reward."

Bork pushed past Steve and Molly to do Kleiber's bidding, and Kleiber moved out of the way.

Steve gasped. Lying naked on the foot-high altar was Ken Anderson. Straps held his hands, ankles, and head steady. Steve fought back nausea.

God damn that woman, he thought. If there is a God in heaven I will return to this earth and kill that Queen Bitch.

Sloat appeared on stage in black silken robes and held *Das Fayden* high in the air for all to see. A cheer rose up. He pranced forward with glee and placed it in a special wrought-iron stand to the side of Lady Eva.

Lady Eva twisted and thumbed through the

275

Das Fayden and then picked up the book. She spoke in words that Steve did not understand, as if reading an incantation.

Several of the gold-robed women dragged Penny forward and tied her down on top of Ken Anderson.

"Oh, Penny," Molly cried out.

Daphne was forced forward and given a silver chalice to drink from. She drank deeply, then the robed ones positioned her over her sister.

Lady Eva reached inside her robe and pulled out a jeweled anthame—the Queen's own witch's knife—and handed it to Daphne, who took it two-handed and raised it high above her head. When she plunged it down at Penny's stomach, Molly screamed, and Steve couldn't help but turn his face away.

Katzmer hated riding in helicopters. If something didn't have wings it shouldn't be able to fly. And here he was flying, along with Senator Dest and three policemen, in the dead black of night toward a mountain in a Huey helicopter.

Everyone in the chopper was armed, and equipped with night-vision gear, including the senator. She had guts, Katzmer had to give her that.

Katzmer was sitting next to one man who had a modified M-14 sniper rifle with a night scope. The man's name tag read, J. Scognamiglio.

"Can you hit anything with that at night?" Katzmer asked him.

Scognamiglio eyed him like he were a worm. "I can knock the butt off a gnat at a thousand yards, bub. How 'bout you?"

"On a good day I hit the bowl when I'm peeing," Katzmer said. "But only if I'm taking a dump at the time."

"Shit," said the sharpshooter.

"Exactly," said Katzmer, smiling and clutching the Uzi one of the sheriff's S.W.A.T. teams had begrudgingly loaned him.

The senator had gone to work fast on the telephone, and they had lucked out. A DEA team was working the area and had night-sight dope finding equipment. That chopper was scanning the mountain looking for evidence of a cavern.

The one they were riding in was a S.W.A.T. copter. Katzmer saw the pilot's lips move, he had said something, and the door gunner cupped his headphones, then leaned toward the others and shouted over the chopper noise: "DEA found a bunch of cars out in the woods, and those two vans you described, but no people. A cave could be keeping them out of sight. We're heading for it, estimate three minutes arrival."

"Lock and load," shouted Scognamiglio.

Katzmer chambered a round automatically, as did the other members in the chopper's bay.

The door gunner manned a spotlight and turned it on when he saw the DEA chopper up ahead. He directed the beam under the other chopper and dropped it to the ground. Something swooped through the beam, and Katzmer caught sight of it. It was a winged thing!

"Shoot it!" he screamed at Scognamiglio. "Shoot it!"

Katzmer dropped his night-vision goggles over his eyes and through the artificially green-tinged night he saw one of the winged things flying away from the DEA chopper and then gain altitude and come back above it. In its claws it held a large rock. It tucked and dove at the chopper and released the rock with deadly accuracy, spreading its wings at the last minute, banked and escaped the chopper's rotors.

The DEA chopper careened on its side and dropped straight down to the ground, crashing and bursting into bright orange flames.

Scognamiglio opened fire on the distant creature, just as the chopper banked, and a second creature had beat the rotor-wash from the chopper and clamped on the right skid and was pulling itself up and into the chopper.

Katzmer leaned forward and around Scognamiglio and in a burst of Uzi fire blew the thing's head off. It dropped away into the night. "I'd say we found the cave," he said, and the chopper started its descent toward the caverns. In the distance, Katzmer saw the line of police cars, red and blue lights flashing pulling into the parking area of the cars.

"I hope we're not too late, Dr. Katzmer," the

278

senator said, and Katzmer shook his head signifying worry. "I hope not, too."

Grandma Lottie was speaking to Daphne, only somehow, it wasn't Grandma Lottie, because she was dead. But none the less it was her voice, maybe like a recording, Daphne wasn't sure, but she was obeying as best she could. Like when the nasty man gave her the chalice before she was led on stage. Mommy had told her to drink, that it would numb her, but Grandma Lottie's voice said, "Don't drink! Pretend to drink!" And she had done just that.

And as they led her out and tied poor Penny on top of the man and given Daphne the chalice she faked drinking deep again, then raised the knife high above her head and plunged it down at Penny-Peanut, turning at the last moment and driving the knife deep into the nearest gold-robed woman. She screamed and blood spurted out all over.

Daphne ran toward Lady Eva, but Sloat intercepted her. She stabbed him, but he didn't flinch. He reached down and pinned her arms to her side. "You were going to die next anyway, little girl."

Daphne struggled but knew she was caught. She bit Sloat's arm. Again he didn't cry out. She heard her mother call out to her . . . and then she began to smell orange blossom, the way she always did before she had one of her fits. She

279

looked over at her mother, heard Grandma Lottie say something unintelligible . . . and then began to cough. Her eyes felt heavy, like they always did before the fit and she felt a heightened sense of vision and then she began to convulse, and even Sloat, who was strong, could not hold her still.

And things began to break the way they always do. Only this time, Daphne was glad, very glad.

Steve turned back to the scene when he heard the scream and realized that something had gone wrong with Lady Eva's plans.

He saw Sloat grab Daphne, and he began to shuffle forward, Molly beside him. And then Daphne began to convulse. Steve and Molly's shackles burst open. Steve's men were freed the same way, and they sprang for their weapons. Lady Eva sprinted toward the back exit and disappeared. Sloat pushed Daphne forward and ran to follow Lady Eva.

Steve heard a great cracking noise and looked up. The water and gas mains that ran across the ceiling had ruptured. Suddenly large chunks of cave ceiling dropped, and the followers, stunned at first began to scream.

Paoletti strapped on a flamethrower, ignited the pilot light, and sprayed fire all over the front row of witches. Screeches followed and the faithful started loping back toward the front entrance.

Baker and Black grabbed their M-16's and sprayed after them.

Steve called over to Paoletti to watch the fire, pointed out that the gas main had been ruptured, then went to untie Ken Anderson. Molly had already rescued Penny.

"It's okay with the flame," Paoletti said. "The room's got to fill with the gas some more before it'll be at flash point, but we better be getting our butts out of here."

"Steve," Molly said urgently. "You asked how to kill a witch? Fire, Steve. Fire. Burn the witch. Burn her! Her territory has been desecrated now—her power diminished greatly. Burn her. She knows she vulnerable, that's why she ran." She pointed at the other flamethrower.

Ken seemed dazed and unsure of where he was. Steve waved Terry Black over. "Make sure he gets out of here and take Molly and the girls too."

"Indubitably," Black joked, which was his way of handling fear. He looked over his shoulder and fired a burst of bullets at some foolhardy followers. They dropped in their tracks.

"Just get them out of here and make sure they are safe."

Steve dropped down to the weapons and pulled Katzmer's duffel back up to him and opened it and pulled out two witch needles. He stuck them in his belt and strapped on a flame-thrower.

Paoletti tossed him a light, and he adjusted the jet and lit the pilot. He gripped the wand in a ready-to-fire position and, not looking back at Molly or the girls, went hunting for the witch.

He knew that there was a maze of tunnels, but guessed she would head back to her chambers and so he proceeded that way. He was sur-prised not to have Cutter and Radd to contend with. Maybe they had gone with Kleiber to fight the backup unit.

God bless Katzmer, he thought. And Senator Dest.

He would save any other blessings. He wasn't out of the woods, yet. He reached Lady Eva's chambers and found her with her back to him, rooting through her closet. He stood by the en-trance, deciding best how to do this, when Sloat screamed and launched himself from behind onto Steve and knocking him to the ground.

Steve saw Lady Eva run towards him as he struggled to rid himself of Sloat, and Sloat's cold dead hands on his throat. Steve half-rolled and freed a witch needle and drove it into Sloat's chest. Sloat screamed, and rolled off. Smoke began rising up off him and by then Lady Eva had reached him.

She shrieked and dove at him.

He struck out with the flamethrower wand and caught her in the temple. She stumbled backward, and looked confused. Steve scrambled to his feet and backed up as she charged again.

He raised the wand and pulled the trigger, and liquid fire sprayed out over her. She screeched and screeched. Steve sidestepped and backed away from her as, enveloped in flames she staggered around the room.

Steve turned quickly, pointed the wand and lit up Sloat, too.

"Bastard," Steve said, and turned back to Lady Eva. She reached out with a fiery hand, and pleaded, "Steve, help me. Help me."

Steve pulled out the second witch needle and threw it at her, but it didn't stick. He hosed her down with flame again and again.

She stopped staggering and dropped to her knees, then reached out toward him, and fell forward, lying dead still, flames consuming her with every passing second.

Steve wanted to stay and watch but he remembered the ruptured gas main in the ceiling, and knew he had to get out of there. He couldn't go back the way he came, there wasn't enough time.

He wasn't sure what to do, then he remembered Lady Eva had spoken of a back entrance where they might take a walk one night. Her private entrance. He unbuckled the flamethrower, let it fall to the ground, and ran toward his best recollection of where that exit tunnel had been.

He smelled gas, but was that smell from the flamethrower or the broken main? He couldn't be sure which. He ran back past the cells to the pits, took the proper tunnel and found a smaller tunnel. He ducked through it. He was sure of the smell of natural gas, now, and he knew that if he didn't get out of there soon, he was going to cook with the rest of those who were left in the caverns.

As he hurried though, he thought, that at least Molly and the girls were safe. He pushed on and came to two tunnels, he chose the left one and pressed on, and suddenly found himself out in the cold night air. He stepped from behind a big rock, and saw a helicopter crashed and burning on the ground, not forty yards away.

He exited left and ran and ran and ran. And when the explosion came it shook the earth and knocked him to the ground.

Twenty-eight

LOOSE ENDS

Steve made his way around the hill following the landing of several helicopters. It brought him to where the cars were parked, and he came up to the sea of whirling emergency lights of the various police agencies.

He was challenged once, but Senator Dest vouched for him and he was allowed to search around for his men. He found Katzmer, and thanked him, and finally, his own first team, standing around. "It was easy to tell the good guys from the bad here," Baker was saying. "You naked, you're bad."

The other guys laughed and Steve asked, "You seen Black and the woman and girls?"

"Yes," said Paoletti, "over there."

Brandner said, "Ken Anderson's in the ambulance, that away. Did you hear the explosion?"

"I experienced it first hand."

Paoletti said: "Tell the powers that be not to

go in. That gas is still being piped in and when it builds back up to critical mass, it's going to blow again, if someone so much as farts wrong."

Steve pointed to Senator Dest. "Go tell her." He looked at his men. "Did you get any word on Kay Audette or Munzo's brother? Did you see them in there?"

The guys mumbled in the negative, and Steve felt a lump in his throat. "Okay," he said, and headed over to a rock where Molly and the girls sat. Terry Black was trying to pick up on her, and Steve interrupted: "She's taken Terry. Thanks for watching them for me."

"Sure," he said, and gave Molly a mischievous smile. He picked up his rifle and headed over to the others.

Daphne and Penny hopped off the rock and ran to him. He bent over and hugged them. Molly stood up and walked forward. "I don't know what to say."

"Say you love me, and I'll be happy."

Molly grinned, scooted forward and hugged him tightly. "I can't believe we got out of that alive," she said, and laid her head on his chest.

"We paid a price, though," said Steve.

They stood there in silence, all of them, holding each other, for a very long time.

On a ledge on the neighboring mountain, the

night wind stirred restlessly, and an owl examined the darkness with his hunter's eyes.

He saw nothing of importance, but stretched his wings and flew out over the valley anyway away from the east, away from the burning helicopter. He sensed, rather than saw that danger was coming.

A flutter of bigger wings filled the night and two flying Hadesmorphs landed on the cliffs.

Lady Eva crawled off Cutter's back. Radd had been killed by the interlopers. Sloat slid down off Gilbey's back.

"We are doomed, Mother."

"Shut up, Sloat."

She stood at the lip of the cliff and watched the burning copter and the light show from the interlopers' police cars in the distance. Her anger rose in her throat, and she forced it down.

She turned and climbed up on Cutter's back. Sloat regained Gilbey's back.

"Do you think they'll figure it out, Mother?" Sloat asked.

"You mean about that Kay Audette and that man-spy that Steve Brogan sent?"

"Yes."

"I don't know. But let it be a lesson to you. No matter how powerful you become always prepare for the worst."

She gripped Cutter's broad shoulders and thought how wise it had been of her to transform Kay Audette into a Hadesmorph duplicate of herself, and that man-spy into a duplicate of Sloat, too.

She knew that they had filled their purpose, and died for her. She could feel it, in the same magical way she could feel the life growing inside her even though it was only a few hours old.

But she and Sloat were alive and free to build and grow powerful again. And after all, that was what was most important.

And of course, she thought, as she kicked Cutter in the sides, and he flapped his great wings and they lifted off, I still have Steve Brogan to woo again, when the Season of the Witch cycles through once more. But for the time being, I will relish the thought of his child growing within me. I have that to keep me warm, and remind me of the day when we will be reunited once again.